**'Tell me what's the matter.'
Urgently he searched her face.**

Boyd reached down to take hold of her hand, and as he did so it went nerveless, and the earrings rolled out of her grasp.

'What the hell is going on here? Why didn't your brother have the guts to come to me and confess he'd taken the diamonds?' he demanded.

'Robbie had nothing to do with it.'

'Oh, stop it!' Boyd said, as though he'd totally run out of patience. How formidable he looked. How handsome! He had taken off his jacket but he was still in his evening clothes, the collar of his white shirt undone, his black dress tie hanging loose.

'Someone's coming!' Leona gave a terrified gasp. She looked towards the entrance hall.

Boyd didn't reply. He grabbed her, hauling her back against the green and gold curtains. 'Kiss me,' he ordered bluntly. 'Kiss me and make it good!

Welcome to the intensely emotional world of

Margaret Way

where rugged, brooding bachelors meet their
match in the burning heart of Australia...

Praise for the author:

THE AUSTRALIAN'S SOCIETY BRIDE

BY
MARGARET WAY

MILLS & BOON
Pure reading pleasure™

First published in Great Britain 2008
Paperback edition 2009
Harlequin Mills & Boon Limited,
Eton House, 18-24 Paradise Road, Richmond, Surrey TW9 1SR

© Margaret Way, Pty., Ltd 2008

ISBN: 978 0 263 86922 4

Set in Times Roman 12¾ on 14 pt
02-0209-54691

Printed and bound in Spain
by Litografia Rosés, S.A., Barcelona

Margaret Way, a definite Leo, was born and raised in the subtropical River City of Brisbane, capital of the Sunshine State of Queensland. A Conservatorium-trained pianist, teacher, accompanist and vocal coach, she found her musical career came to an unexpected end when she took up writing, initially as a fun thing to do. She currently lives in a harbourside apartment at beautiful Raby Bay, a thirty-minute drive from the state capital, where she loves dining *al fresco* on her plant-filled balcony, overlooking a translucent green marina filled with all manner of pleasure craft—from motor cruisers costing millions of dollars and big, graceful yachts with carved masts standing tall against the cloudless blue sky, to little bay runabouts. No one and nothing is in a mad rush, so she finds the laid-back village atmosphere very conducive to her writing. With well over 100 books to her credit, she still believes her best is yet to come.

Recent books by the same author:

BRIDE AT BRIAR'S RIDGE*
WEDDING AT WANGAREE VALLEY*
CATTLE RANCHER, SECRET SON

CHAPTER ONE

"LEO, YOU KNOW they don't want me, but they feel obliged to ask me," Robbie, her stepbrother said. As usual, he was making himself comfortable, lolling back on her brand-new sofa, dark head on a cushion, his long legs slung languidly over the other end.

This was a familiar theme between them, causing Leona, always the peacemaker, to answer automatically, "You know that's not true." Sadly, it *was* true. "You're good company, Robbie. You're an asset to any house party. Besides, you're on Boyd's polo team, which counts for a lot, and you're a darn good tennis player—my best doubles partner. We can and do beat the rest of them." The rest of them being the close-knit Blanchard clan, many of whom would be attending the weekend house party.

"Except Boyd," Robbie chipped in. "Now, Boyd is a man to marvel over—a business dynamo, IQ off the charts, superb athlete, a serious heartthrob with the women. What more could a man hope for? They could have cast him as the new James Bond."

"Forget Boyd," said Leona. "I rather like the new guy." As always, she was masking the deep feelings she had for Boyd—feelings she thought she would never get past—as she chucked a cushion at Robbie. "Though I will concede they don't come any more perfect than Boyd." This was said very dryly.

Robbie laughed, deftly fielding the silk cushion and depositing it on the floor. "Sure you don't actually love him?" He lifted his head to flash her a bright challenging look. Robbie was teeming with intuition and he frequently caught her out.

"Now, that would be a turn-up, wouldn't it?" she answered, hoping her white skin wasn't showing tell-tale bright flags of colour. "He *is* my second cousin."

"Well, not strictly speaking. You'd have to give or take a few 'steps'," Robbie reminded her. "There've been so many deaths, divorces and re-marriages in the Blanchard family."

That was certainly true. Triumph and tragedy aplenty. She and Boyd, for instance, had both lost their mothers. She when she was eight. His beautiful mother, Alexa, had become Leona's honorary aunt after that until she'd died when Boyd was in his mid-twenties. Boyd's father, Rupert, Chairman of Blanchards, had remarried two years later, not to a nice sensible woman somewhere near his own age, as the family had dared to hope, but to a flamboyant divorcee, the daughter of one of Rupert's old cronies who sat on the Board of Blanchards. She was just a handful of years older than Rupert's only son and heir, Boyd.

The family had been reduced to a state of shock at the speed of the new alliance. Robbie privately referred to the newcomer as the Bride of Frankenstein. And he wasn't the only one in the family to gloat. Most expected the marriage would end in a ferocious court battle and a huge settlement. All had the great good sense to keep their opinions to themselves, except Geraldine, Rupert's older unmarried sister who didn't hesitate to speak her mind, as befitted her position. Despite that, Rupert had married his Jinty—short for Virginia—regardless. Rupert Blanchard was a law unto himself. And so, as it had transpired, was Jinty.

"Anyway, we're not talking about Boyd, we're talking about *you*," Leona picked up the conversation. "Why you keep writing yourself off, I don't know."

"Ah, but you *do* know, Leo." Robbie sighed. "Low self-esteem." The unhappy, rebellious six-year-old he had been when Leona had first laid eyes on him fourteen years before glittered out of his dark eyes. "The problem is, I don't know *who*

I am. Carlo didn't want any part of me. Didn't even bother to toss a coin for me. 'Heads me, tails your mother'. *Your* dad, my stepfather, is a good man, a gentleman of the old school, but he still doesn't know what to make of me. Just hopes things don't get any worse. Mother dearest has never loved me. No need to ask why. I don't make her proud and I don't look a scrap like her. I keep reminding her of Carlo and their failed marriage. To top it off, I'm *not* a Blanchard, am I, all these years later?" Robbie's intense young face took on a bitter cast. "I'm the misfit in your midst, the emotionally neglected adopted son."

In a way he was absolutely spot on, but Leona didn't hold back on the groans. "Please, Robbie, not again!" She allowed her still coltish frame to collapse into an armchair opposite him, feeling weighed down by her constant anxiety for him and his well-being. "Do you really have to sprawl all over my new sofa?" she asked, not really minding. As usual Robbie was immaculate, very sharply groomed and dressed. Nothing scruffy about Robbie, not that it would have been tolerated. Robbie, for all his moans, well knew on which side his bread was buttered.

"How can I not?" he responded, not moving an inch. "It's so darn comfortable. You have superb taste, Leo. You're a super girl altogether. Best of all, you're as tender-hearted as you're beautiful.

Lord knows how I would have made it in this family without you—my big sister, my most trusted confidante and supporter. You're the only one who doesn't think I'll turn out a rogue like Carlo."

"No, no!" she automatically denied.

"Yes, yes!" said Robbie. "They're all just waiting for me to prove it. Probably the best thing I could do, so far as the family is concerned, is fall under a bus."

And he didn't have it all that wrong, Leona thought dismally. For that reason, she couldn't let the opportunity go past. "You might consider your gambling is a worry, Robbie. You have to get a grip on that." She couldn't bring herself to throw in drugs again. Not so soon after their last confrontation. Robbie ran with a fast, moneyed, mostly mindless young crowd, hell-bent on pleasure, or what they considered pleasure, which didn't include work. She knew for a fact he dabbled with pot, like so many of his peers. She was fairly certain it hadn't gone any further than that. Not *yet* anyway. Like her, Robbie carried the burden of the Blanchard name, which meant pressure as well as prestige, power, mega-wealth. But, unlike her, Robbie wasn't the most stable of people.

The only person he seemed to be able to commit to was *her*, his "big sister." They hadn't used the "step" for years and years. Robbie just referred to her as his sister, as she called him her brother. It didn't seem to matter that there was no bond in *blood*. Her father had legally adopted Robbie directly after he'd married Robbie's mother, Delia. Newcomers who didn't know Leona and Robbie's background always commented with perplexed frowns, "But you're not a bit alike." Maybe the fact that Robbie—christened Roberto Giancarlo D'Angelo—strongly resembled his Italian father while she was a porcelain-skinned redhead had something to do with it.

"Pure art nouveau," Boyd had long since labelled her looks, consigning her to the romantic, overly sentimental Pre-Raphaelite lot—the willowy springtime woodland nymph with her loosely pinned mane of red-gold hair, flowing floral diaphanous dress, away with the fairies. Not his usual cup of tea—slick, elegant, the perfect brunette, all long legs and womanly curves, whereas she had as many curves as her ironing-board.

Don't think of Boyd.

It was excellent advice. She'd do well to follow it. Even being around him was dangerous enough.

Robbie's voice brought her out of her discomfiting thoughts. "I promise you I will, Leo. Have there been more whisperings about me in the family? 'What else is Robbie doing'?" he mimicked a female family voice.

There had been plenty of those, she thought. Shocked horror from the older generation. Delia, his mother, reduced to fat crocodile tears over her son's misconduct. "Remember there's Boyd to consider. Nothing gets past him, Robbie. He has eyes and ears everywhere."

"Spies, spooks!" Robbie laughed as if it was funny. It wasn't. Robbie sustained himself with cynical, sometimes bitter banter, when in reality Boyd Blanchard was everything he yearned to be. "Scion of generations of multi-millionaires, now billionaires," he continued, dangling an arm to the floor. "Now there's a man for you."

"Oh, I don't know." Leona pursed her finely cut, sensitive lips.

"Come off it." Robbie grinned wickedly and swung upright with the strength and elegance of the university champion gymnast he was. "Maybe he's the one to awaken you—"

"He is *not*!" Leona protested, uncharacteristically cross.

"Well, you do a good job of covering up, but I *know* you, remember? You admire him as much as everyone else. Problematic old me included. He might bawl me out from time to time, but I know he means well by me. I'm simply not in his league. He's cast in the heroic mould. I'm the one everyone is waiting to see unravel. No wonder Boyd is worshipped by the family. He's probably the most eligible bachelor in the country, all the women love him, not yet thirty—"

"He is. A month ago," Leona confirmed, not giving Robbie a chance to go on. Counting off Boyd's attributes was a sure way to madness.

"Fancy that! I wasn't invited to the party, then?"

"There was *no* party. He was much too busy."

"Well, that would be true enough." Robbie was always fair. "He's a workaholic. Just think what he's achieved. He's ready to step into Rupert's shoes right now. Boyd and Jinty—one of my least favourite women, as I've told you umpteen times—are the only ones in the entire clan who don't go in fear and awe of old Rupe. And there's *you*," he pondered thoughtfully. "The odd thing is, the ruthless old devil is very fond of *you*. That's the only thing about him I like. He despises me."

"Not true." Again Leona shook her red-gold head when she knew the autocratic Rupert considered Robbie "worthless". "He's ready to take you into the firm as soon as you complete your degree."

And why not? Robbie was very clever and he was right about one thing: Rupert had always shown a marked interest in her since she was a little girl. Intimidating with most people, he had always been very gentle with her, especially after she had lost her mother, Serena, in that fatal riding accident on the Brooklands estate. In those far off days

Boyd, six years her elder, vividly handsome and clever, already at fourteen six feet tall, had made a special effort to take her under his wing as if she were a stray fluffy duckling. He had always looked after her at family functions and gatherings, without any need for prompting. He had just done it. In those days Boyd had been her hero. She told herself she had long run out of hero worship. These days, Boyd affected her so powerfully, so painfully, she could scarcely make eye contact with him. He made her nervous and excited. He challenged her and honed her already sharp wits. It was torture to be physically near him, yet she couldn't seem to draw back. The fact was, she was mesmerised by his whole persona—those piercing, incredibly beautiful blue eyes that wooed as they wounded. She was a seething mass of contradictions where Boyd was concerned. He stirred her and she feared him. Any liaison between her and Boyd would never be accepted. Not that he had ever looked at her in that way. Well, how did he look at her, exactly? Sometimes he made her feel extraordinarily *beautiful*. Inside and out. Other times he seemed to go out of his way to alienate her. The cool tongue. The blazing eyes. Face it: it was *her* fantasy, not his.

Robbie broke into her errant thoughts again. "I expect I get invited because they want to keep an eye on me."

"Same way they keep an eye on all of us," she said with a smile.

"Just like royalty! At least they acknowledge you for the clever, creative young woman you are. The fact you're a genuine beauty is always an enormous help, and you have the wonderful gift of being able to get on with all sorts of people."

"Except Boyd." The fact she had voiced it aloud made her twitch with self-disgust.

Robbie laughed. "I expect there's a very good reason for that. I ask myself—all that sparring the two of you go on with. Are you both playing a part? Is it all a sham?"

"Funny sort of sham." She spoke as though the very idea of being secretly in love with Boyd was utterly ridiculous. "We bring out the worst in each other." How proficient she had grown at crushing down all other explanations. It was bad enough they lurked on the outskirts of her brain.

"Personally, I think you're a good match," Robbie announced as though he had given it serious consideration. "Boyd needs a woman with fiery red hair. You're good at keeping him in line. Well, I'd best be off."

"I hope that doesn't mean to the races." Leona stood up. It was Saturday and the Spring Carnival was underway.

A little colour rose to Robbie's olive cheeks. "I don't do much harm. I'm taking Deb. Barrington and his current squeeze are coming along. Just a fun afternoon and a chance for the girls to dress up. I'm surprised you're not going. Old Rupe's glamour two-year-old is bound to win its race. Shall I put a couple of bob on for you?"

Leona shook her head, her beautiful hair loosely caught back in a high knot. "I've never felt the slightest urge to gamble, Robbie. With money, that is. I certainly play my hunches. That's the right side of my brain. Money makes money for the likes of Rupert." She planted an affectionate kiss on Robbie's cheek. He wasn't tall and she was for a woman. "If I were you, I'd put my boot down firmly on what you've got." Robbie was on a generous allowance from her father but she knew he made short work of it. He often borrowed from her, promising he would pay her back. Sometimes he did. More often he didn't.

The two of them walked to the door of Leona's very attractive open-plan apartment, which took full advantage of its marvellous location overlooking Sydney Harbour. The apartment had been a twenty-first birthday present from "The Family". It was their way of showing their approval of the way she conducted herself and brought credit to the family name. No way could she have afforded it herself, although with her latest promotion to personal assistant to Beatrice Caldwell, a fashion icon and overall Director of Blanchards Fashion, she had now hit an income high.

"You deserve it, girl. Like me, you have the eye!"

High praise from the autocratic and incredibly difficult to please Beatrice.

"So you *are* coming to the house party?" Leona needed to double-check. "You're expected to reply." Good manners ranked high on the Blanchard expectations list.

"*Naturellement!* And that just about exhausts my French for the day. Just for *you*, Leo. No one else."

"Don't be difficult, sweetie." She hugged him in the sisterly, protective way she had with him.

"Maybe if Carlo had stuck around instead of abandoning me," Robbie suggested unhappily. "But he couldn't wait to get back to Italy, remarry, father several more children."

"Let's hope he's done a better job with them than he did with you." Leona's tone was uncharacteristically hard. Was it any wonder her heart ached for Robbie? How could she not recognise his *emptiness*? Delia appeared to feel little or nothing for her only child, incredible as that seemed. Perhaps, if Robbie had taken after Delia—blonde, blue-eyed…? Carlo D'Angelo had never contacted his first born over the years, much less invited him to visit and meet his half-siblings. "It's *his* loss, Robbie," she said, resorting to a brisk confident tone. "Believe in yourself, like I do." Robbie had to buck up. With her hand resting on his arm, she thought she detected an inner agitation he wasn't allowing her to see.

"Everything okay?" She frowned. "You would tell me if it weren't?"

"Everything's fine!" Robbie gave a brief laugh. "Well, then, Leo love, next time I'll see you will be next weekend at Brooklands."

She smiled back. "Bring your racket. We'll lick 'em, same as always."

"Satisfying, isn't it?" he smirked.

"Very."

If only everything *was* fine, Robbie thought dismally as he strolled off to the lift. All sorts of anxieties were settling heavily in his stomach. Leo was wonderful. He loved her dearly. The only one in the world he did love, actually. In the end he hadn't had it in him to ask her for another loan. Hadn't he already asked enough of her? In fact he still owed her. But he was desperately in need of money and, to be honest, becoming increasingly frightened of the people he had got involved with. Basically, they were thugs, even if they moved freely through high society. God knew what they might do to him if he couldn't keep them happy. Or happy enough. He had the horrible feeling a trap was closing around him. Leo was right. His love of gambling, yet another unfortunate trait he had inherited from Carlo—were there any good ones?—had pitched him headlong into a maelstrom of danger. Old Rupe's brilliant two-year-old—Blazeaway—was practically guaranteed a win this afternoon. He'd put the few thousand he had left on its nose.

Characteristically, Robbie shrugged off his nightmares and began to whistle an old tune to keep up his spirits.

CHAPTER TWO

ON THE FOLLOWING Saturday morning Leona decided to let the parade of Blanchards get away from the city before she started out on her drive to the Blanchards' splendid country estate. In one way she was thrilled to be going back—she adored the house and its magnificent gardens and parkland, spreading over several square kilometres—in another, meeting up with Boyd again left her unsettled in mind and body. It seemed an age since she had seen him, in reality, just over a month, but he had been overseas on family business. Since Rupert had reached his sixties with such a splendid heir, the older man was happy to spend a lot more time at Brooklands. The result was that the mantle of power and responsibility had fallen more heavily on Boyd's shoulders.

Then again, Boyd knew all about power and taking over the reins. He had been groomed for the role. There had never been the possibility, or even the fear, that he might not possess his father's brilliant business brain; or when the time came, that he might opt out of a lifetime of hard work and enormous responsibility. Such a life might not have appealed to him. With a lavish trust fund set up by his grandfather, Boyd could simply have walked away and enjoyed a life of leisure, doing anything he wanted—Lord knew he was clever enough—but Boyd had shown even in his early teens that he was more than capable of bearing the burdens of a great business empire. His ambition, to the family's immense relief, was to continue his forebears' achievements.

Everything Boyd tackled he did with brilliance and determination, she thought, fixing her eyes on the road ahead. He was far more than a chip off the old block. Boyd, if the truth be told, was Rupert's superior in every way. Certainly he had that wonderful *polish* he had inherited from Alexa, along with her stunning sapphire eyes. At just turned thirty, he was right on top of his game, on course to outperform Rupert and the original family fortune builders and their achievements. Boyd commanded genuine liking, love and respect, whereas Rupert was rather more famous for commanding fear.

Extraordinary, then, that Rupert had taken such a fancy to *her*. The one time Rupert had ever been seen to break down was at her mother's funeral, when a stiff upper lip at his own wife's funeral had prevailed. Extremely odd, that. She remembered Alexa, a close friend of her mother, always so poised, had been in floods of tears that day too. Even as a stunned and grief-stricken little girl she'd remembered.

A wonderful rider, her mother, Serena, had broken her neck in a freak fall, taking an old stone wall at the upper reaches of the Brooklands lake. It was a wall she had jumped dozens of times before. Only that last time she and her horse had taken a catastrophic tumble. It was later discovered the horse's hoof had snagged in a strong loop of ivy clinging to the wall.

Sixteen years ago, Leona thought with familiar sadness. Sixteen years I've been without my mother. She still remembered how her mother had bent to kiss her before she had gone out on her ride.

"Won't be long, my darling. When I come back, we'll all go for a nice long swim."

Serena didn't know—couldn't know—she wouldn't be coming back. Not alive, anyway.

The entire family had taken her mother's death badly. Serena had been so deeply mourned that it seemed there had been no love left over for Delia, her successor, her father's second wife. The family had considered no one good enough to replace Serena. Certainly not Delia, who had "ambushed" her grieving father, bringing with her a difficult small son to boot. Perhaps that was why she, Leona, was held close to the Blanchard core. She wasn't a member of the main family. But she *was* the image of her mother. That seemed to accord her a special grace.

The great wrought iron gates to the estate were standing open. A mile long private road led to the house. Magnificent trees of an immense height lined the way, their outermost branches interlocking so that the road beneath formed a wonderful golden-green tunnel.

Minutes later, she was out of the tunnel and driving over an arched stone bridge that spanned the shimmering green lake. Fed by an underground river, the lake, very deep in some places, spread out over three acres, dotted here and there with picturesque little islands, which had become the breeding grounds for wild duck and other waterfowl. Today a flotilla of black swans sailed under the bridge. The lake's calm waters, glassy green with a multitude of flashing silvers, were spectacularly fringed by deep banks of pure white arum lilies, Japanese purple iris and a wealth of other aquatic plants.

Up ahead was the house. Built in the style of an English manor house, with various extensions added over the years in the same style, it had evolved into a very grand property indeed. A vast sweep of lawn and formal gardens lay before it, the whole estate surrounded by undulating hills and valleys, brooks and streams. When she was a child she had counted the rooms—thirty-two, including a beautiful big ballroom where many large family and charity functions had been held over the years. Alexa had made the annual Brooklands Garden Party one of the most memorable events on the social calendar, a feat Jinty had never attempted to emulate. The glorious grounds were ideal for the purpose.

No one could match Alexa, Leona thought. It was a tragedy she had died so young. She had often pondered her private belief that Alexa had not been at all happy in her marriage but the subject had never been broached. In public Rupert and Alexa had played the role of the perfect couple. It was only as Leona had grown to womanhood that she'd begun to sense the very real *distance* between the two. They'd practically lived their lives apart, although Alexa had obviously decided to make the best of her marriage, always looking out for her beloved son, and applying her considerable skills and energies to running a large estate and numerous charities close to her heart.

If a woman like that couldn't have her happy ever after, forget the romantics, she thought. Marriage was a *huge* risk.

The presence of water was everywhere at Brooklands. The many brooks on the estate had, in fact, given it its name. Water was magic.

Way off to Leona's right were the three polo fields, covering a huge area given that one polo field had an area equivalent to ten football fields. The boundaries of the fields were deeply shaded by massive plantings of trees, both natives and exotics weaving in and out of one another. A world-famous landscaper had been brought in by Boyd's great-grandparents, who had determined on and succeeded in creating a world class garden. Many years on, another celebrity landscaper had worked with Rupert when he'd decided he wanted polo fields on the estate. A splendid polo player in his day, Rupert now left it to Boyd to carry on the tradition. Boyd freely admitted he found the dangerous, fast paced sport great relaxation.

A match had been organised for Sunday afternoon with a visiting team. Though he was a marvellously dashing player, she always found herself praying that Boyd would not be harmed. It was such a fast, rough game, though very thrilling for the spectator, especially those who adored horses.

All of them desperately needed Boyd to succeed Rupert. None of the other male cousins, even the really clever ones, and there were quite a few, could possibly take his place.

Even as she thought of him, she was conscious of a kind of panic moving through her. Her heart was beating faster. She could feel its mad flutter. The big thing was not to allow her schoolgirl panic to ruin the weekend. Think positive.

Boyd.

Damn, damn, damn. Just his name did her in. Head and heart. She didn't want it. It wasn't right. The very strength of her feelings made her afraid. Did anyone realise how hard it was for her to act normal around him? Robbie, maybe. But then Robbie saw too much.

At twenty-four, wasn't it high time she started to move past her feelings for Boyd? Give other guys a chance? There were plenty of them standing in line—no doubt the Blanchard name was an added attraction. But she was no heiress. She was one of the worker bees. It was a terrifying feeling to be held in thrall, for that was how she had come to think of it. It was every bit as bad an addiction as Robbie's gambling.

She wondered if Boyd was still seeing Ally McNair. Ally was lovely and great fun. There had been Zoe Renshaw before Ally. Jemma Stirling. Not to forget Holly Campbell. She hadn't liked Holly. Such a snob. And, of course, there was Chloe Compton, heiress to another great retailing fortune, therefore judged by Rupert as very suitable.

Everyone in the family liked Chloe, including her. Rupert had gone out of his way to give her his nod of approval. There had barely been a time when Boyd didn't have the most beautiful girls chasing after him. Some, like Ally and Chloe, turned out to be regulars, but Boyd didn't seem in any hurry to commit himself. In any case he was, as Robbie said, a workaholic. Come to that, she worked pretty darn hard herself.

Even her boss had been known to comment on the fact. And Bea hadn't signed her up because she was one of the Blanchard clan. She had been given the job on merit alone. Although many in the country's fashion world would have given their eye teeth to land the job, most of Leona's colleagues found Bea immensely difficult—some days she was chillier than a travelling iceberg—but all in all Leona liked and greatly admired her boss. Bea was a huge driving force in fashion, and her own personal guru, and Leona knew in her bones that one day—all right, it was years off—she would be able to take over from Bea.

Jinty made a theatrical business of greeting her— hugging and kissing her with practised insincerity. "Lovely to have you with us again, Leo," she gushed. "Your outfit is perfect." Jinty's large, rather hard china-blue eyes comprehensively studied Leona from head to toe. "You know precisely what fashion is all about. But of course you have that extraordinary figure. What I wouldn't do to be as skinny as you!"

"Give up the champagne, Jinty?" Leona suggested with a teasing smile, knowing Jinty's big show of affection was sadly all an act. Everything was an act with sexy, bosomy Jinty, including her marriage. In the very next instant, as expected, Leona was waved away as of no consequence as Jinty's eyes flashed towards the door, brilliant with expectation. Instantly Leona had the gut feeling that it was Boyd arriving. Boyd was of infinitely more interest than she could ever hope to be. Boyd, the family superstar. She realised he must have left Sydney not long after her.

As though someone was physically shoving her in the back, Leona hurried up the grand sweep of the staircase. She wasn't ready to meet up with Boyd yet. Maybe she never would be.

She was in the same room she usually occupied. It had its own bathroom and a small sitting room— more a suite than just a bedroom. She had loved this room in the old days but Jinty, once installed in a position of power, had decided that new brides had a pressing obligation to sweep clean. At least Rupert had stopped her from doing anything much on the ground floor, with its beautiful welcoming reception rooms and library, but she had been given carte blanche on the upper floor. As a consequence Jinty had suffered a wild reaction. She had gone about her task like a woman possessed.

To the collective family mind, a kind of chaos had broken out—a chaos nurtured by unlimited money. It had also laid waste to the true elegance and country comfort of what had gone before. Now everything was *sumptuous!* Her spacious, high ceilinged bedroom was a prime example of Jinty's love of the baroque. There were lashings of gilt, lashings of Louis, lashings of ornamentation, damasks and silks. She fully expected to one day see a reflection of Marie Antoinette in the ornately gilded circular mirror. What the revamp lacked in style it more than made up for in a superfluity of riches. Money was no object and Jinty didn't need a good reason to spend.

There was a tap on the door and Leona turned to see Hadley, a permanent member of the household staff, smiling at her. Hadley—Eddie to her—was a big, pleasant-faced man with hands the size of dinner plates and a shock of thick tawny hair only now turning silver. He was holding her suitcase and another small piece of luggage. "Where would you like them, Miss Leo?"

"Please…just beside the bed, thanks, Eddie. All's well with you?"

"No complaints, apart from my sciatica that comes and goes. I'm pushing sixty, you know." He deposited her luggage, then stood upright, looking around him with the kind of baffled awe that most people viewed Jinty's efforts.

"And you don't look anything like it," Leona said, which was perfectly true. "Was that Boyd I heard arriving?"

"Indeed it was," Hadley remarked dryly, trusting to Leona's discretion. "A great favourite with his stepmother is Mr Boyd." A conclusion the entire family and staff had long since arrived at. "Mrs Blanchard's sister, Tonya, is here as well."

For a moment Leona looked at him in complete dismay. "Not Tonya?" She felt a silent scream of protest start up inside her head.

"Someone must have thought it was a lovely idea," Hadley murmured, tongue in cheek. Tonya was a very demanding and unpopular guest at Brooklands.

It couldn't have been Boyd, Leona thought. She had once overheard Boyd telling his father after one particularly strained dinner party, for which he blamed Tonya's abrasive tongue, that he didn't want her in the house any more. Tonya was a born troublemaker, a malicious one at that, churning out gossip and a whole lot of misinformation at every possible opportunity. As Jinty's sister, she swanned about the estate, treating the staff as though they were invisible. Added to that, she made no bones about the fact that she found Boyd enormously attractive. What was more, she had deluded herself into thinking she had as good a chance as anyone of landing him. Not that she was getting much encouragement from her sister. Jinty disapproved of her as much as everyone else.

So who was it who had invited Tonya? With a

thrill of horror Leona thought it just might have been Rupert. He had such an alarmingly perverse streak. He had to keep proving to his son that he was still Boss and could invite whom he pleased. Though Rupert adored his heir, in a strange way their relationship was fraught with hidden conflicts and dangers. Leona often thought it was the ghost of Alexa that stood between them—that and Boyd's superior capabilities. On the one hand Boyd's brilliance was a cause of great pride to Rupert, on the other it caused a somewhat irrational level of jealousy and resentment.

Rupert had a monumental ego. Boyd did not.

A buffet lunch was laid out in the informal dining room for those of the family who had arrived. When Leona walked in, golden sunlight was streaming through the huge Palladian windows which allowed marvellous views of the rear gardens. Although there was a terrace outside for extra dining, the informal dining room with so much glass gave Leona the feeling of being outdoors. As the ancestral home of the Blanchard clan, frequently visited by its members, the large room, decorated with a valuable collection of botanical prints, had been set with a number of glass-topped circular tables on carved timber bases, specially carved in the Philippines. Each table easily seated eight on handsome upholstered rattan armchairs, rather than having one very long extension table as in the formal dining room. It had all been Alexa's idea.

Leona, who'd had a light breakfast of yoghurt and fruit at around seven a.m., found herself hungry. She was at the fortunate stage of her life when she could eat as much as she liked without putting on an ounce of weight. Good to know, but she stuck pretty religiously to the right foods anyway. Fine dark chocolate was her one vice, but she was well on the way to achieving a New Year resolution of only eating a single wickedly delicious piece a day.

At least ten members of the family were there before her, helping themselves to a buffet so lavish that Leona started to think of the world's starving millions. The best restaurant in Sydney couldn't have topped this spread, delivered by a stream of staff from the kitchen. At least the staff got to eat what was left over; it was one of the perks of the job.

"Oh, there you are, Leo!" she was greeted on all sides. Lovely to know that people were happy to see her and she, for the most part, was happy to see them.

Geraldine, who was a fashion icon herself—albeit more than a touch eccentric—was wearing a striking high-rise red hat. She jumped up from the table to come towards Leona with outstretched arms.

"Don't you look beautiful, Leo dear!" They exchanged kisses, blessedly sincere. Shrewd grey eyes searched Leona's face. "Such a pleasure to see you. You grow more and more like your dear mother every day. Come sit beside me. I want to hear all you've been up to."

Leona smiled back. "Just give me a moment to grab some food, Aunty Gerri."

From behind them came a feline little comment, something Tonya was never short of, "Yes, *do*. You're dangerously thin, Leona. Sure you're eating right?"

"Oh, do shut up, Tonya," Geraldine said, as brusque when she chose to be as her brother Rupert.

"Shut up? For heaven's sake." Tonya pretended to gasp, then she fell silent as the atmosphere suddenly heightened.

The reason? Boyd had entered the room.

Here was a man dazzling enough to break any girl's heart, Leona thought.

This love of mine.

The words sprang from the well of truth deep inside her. She couldn't suppress her true feelings. She couldn't choose the time or the place when they surfaced. The one thing she *could* ensure was that they were never exposed. Not to Boyd, whose position alone allowed no access. And especially not to Rupert, who had his own plans for the Crown prince. It was she who had chosen to lay down her heart. That Boyd could love her back in the same way was just an impossible dream.

Nevertheless she couldn't stop herself staring at him. After all, everyone else was. Some inches over six feet, superb physique, a constant tan from the time he spent yachting on the Harbour, an enviable head of thick black hair swept back from a fine brow, elegantly sculpted bones—he would look good at ninety—and those beautiful magnetic eyes, as deep a blue as the finest sapphires in the Crown jewels. Those eyes, inherited from his mother, set him apart.

The big hush seemed endless. It had to be enormously flattering, Leona thought, but Boyd took it in his stride. Probably accepted it as his due. No, that wasn't true. Boyd was no attention seeker. He simply didn't notice it. It was like witnessing a medieval prince coming in from the hunt, the public adoration merely his due. Leona couldn't help a tightening of her facial muscles—a little flare of rebellion? Public capitulation to Boyd's splendid persona was not her thing at all. She enjoyed being the one not to swoon. Besides, she needed a shield to separate her from him. It was the paradox she'd had to live with for years. Behind the mask, the strategies and the countless diversionary tactics she had developed for self-protection, she felt constantly starved for the sight of him.

Where you are, I want to be.

Lyrics of a beautiful song. They were so true.

A smile flared white against the dark tan of his skin. He lifted a nonchalant hand in greeting. "Hi, everyone!"

"Great you're here, Boyd!" came the chorus from the tables.

"We're expecting a cracker game tomorrow!" This from one of the great-uncles. Playing polo was a release for Boyd and they all loved watching him.

Tonya seized the moment by going up to him and laying a proprietorial hand on his arm. A petite, sharp-featured but attractive blonde, she looked like a doll beside him, even in her spike-heeled shoes.

"Cheek of her!" Geraldine muttered, herself grabbing Leona's arm in a surprisingly strong grip. "Doesn't she know she drives him mad?"

"So who invited her?" Leona asked, gently easing her arm out of Geraldine's fierce hold. She had her own suspicions.

"My brother, of course." Geraldine had confirmed them. Geraldine, who often referred to her powerful brother as "the tyrannosaurus" humphed, "Rupert likes to throw a spanner in the works when we all know who the right gel is for Boyd."

The right gel for Boyd?

"Chloe Compton?" Leona hazarded with a profoundly sinking heart.

"Gracious, no!" Geraldine turned on her, almost indignant. "Go fill your plate, child, then come back to me. Is that stepbrother of yours coming?"

"He *was* invited, Gerri. And he is on Boyd's polo team."

"All right, all right, so loyal. Not that I don't admire it." Geraldine shook her elegant silver head so that the little quiff of feathers on the hat which matched her chic suit danced in the breeze. "Matter of fact I quite like him, even if he does have the makings of a bit of a rogue. His father had charm too, but what a dreadful man, running off like that and leaving the boy. Being abandoned doesn't make for little angels."

Words to live by.

And then he was beside her. "How's it going, Flower Face?"

Again the familiar contraction in her breast. The invading warmth in her blood. Even her tongue stuck to the roof of her mouth. For all her strategies, nothing worked. As always, his voice fell with dangerous charm on her too sensitive ears. Sometimes, not often these days, he came out with that moniker, *Flower Face*. Each time it made a flutter of excitement pass over her, as if he'd actually stroked her naked body with a feather. Flower Face was the pet name he had for her when she was growing up. When she was his fluffy stray duckling.

She made herself steady, astonished she could do so. She glanced up, seemingly casual, allowing herself to meet his gaze for mere seconds only. She couldn't for the life of her manage a smile. Within her all was excitement and confusion. Her eyes, had she known it, were a pure crystalline green, set as they were against porcelain skin and the scintillating reds and golds of her long, naturally curly hair.

Deliberately she focused those eyes on his fine cotton shirt, white with a blue stripe, the long sleeves carelessly pushed to the elbow. She could see the tanned skin of his chest, the beginnings of the mat of hair, black as black. Boyd's height and handsomeness was only the half of his extraordinary sexual radiance. She knew other handsome young men but, though they did their best to engage her interest, they were mere schoolboys beside Boyd.

"If you don't like this shirt, I can always change it," he said.

She wanted to slap herself alert. "Actually I was admiring it. Helmut Lang, isn't it?"

"If you say so, Leona, that's good enough for me. You're the fashion expert in the family."

"Don't put yourself down," she scoffed. "Didn't *Icon* magazine name you one of the most stylish men in the country?"

He stared at her in mock astonishment. "You saw that, did you?"

With an effort she ignored the mockery. "Anyway, how was the trip—a big success?" She was pleased she was able to speak so collectedly.

His expression of indulgence abruptly sobered. "In many ways. Deals were done, a few swung. Blanchards has a lot of clout, but nothing is as it seems these days, Leo. It's a dangerous world out there. And becoming increasingly so."

"I know." She bent her head. " Terror and suffering everywhere." She didn't tell him how she worried every time he flew off on one of his many overseas trips. For that matter, she suffered a degree of apprehension on her own overseas buying trips with Bea.

He nodded, looking down at her hair as it caught fire in the sunlight before focusing on the buffet table.

"What are *you* having?" he asked.

"The same as you," she answered tartly, another defence mechanism. One of the things she did to put distance between them because, oddly enough, they had many things in common. They loved horses, country life. They liked the same food, music, books, films, even people. They both shared a great love for Brooklands and they both derived enormous pleasure out of being successful at what they did, finding relaxation there.

He laughed, looking much amused. "Right then. Leave it to me. I know what you like. Go back and join Gerri. Save a place for me on your other side."

Her shimmering eyes ranged across the large room, at the groups of laughing, chattering people, then back to him. "What, with Tonya waving a hand?" Tonya was indeed waving an unrestrained hand, trying to capture Boyd's attention. It was a wonder she wasn't banging a spoon on the table.

"Doesn't give up, does she?" he murmured dryly, blatantly ignoring the summons. "I love it, playing happy families. Do as I say, Leo." He spoke with a natural authority that had nothing to do with arrogance. "I don't get to see enough of you."

On track again, she spoke with a spurt of challenge. "That's an order then, is it?"

He laughed—so annoying, so devastating—before turning to glance at the lavish buffet. "You know what, Flower Face? You've made an art form of challenging me."

"Maybe I'm a rebel at heart," she suggested.

"How could you not be with that glorious red hair?" He picked up two plates. "By the way, do you want to go riding with me this afternoon?"

The offer was so unexpected that she just stood there, overtaken by excitement and shock.

"Well?" Boyd asked, his blue eyes moving lightly over her. What he saw was a lyrically beautiful young woman in an extremely pretty silk dress—pure, virginal and incredibly sexy, which he knew she was unaware of. And for once lost for words.

Silently she willed herself to answer. "I should check that Robbie is okay," she said, not enjoying the nervousness she heard in her voice. Exactly *how* was Boyd looking at her? Whatever was in his mind, it was very unnerving. "He hasn't arrived yet."

"How old is Robbie now?" He shifted his brilliant gaze to the buffet, as though aware of her inner confusion.

"He's still my little brother."

"High time he stood on his own two feet," he said crisply. "This little brother bit has gone on too long."

"And you don't like it?" She leaned towards him, aware that others might be watching—most certainly Tonya—deliberately keeping her tone low.

Boyd too spoke quietly, but forcefully nonetheless. "He uses you, Leo. That's the bit I don't like. He loves you. I'm well aware of that. But you're too vulnerable where Robbie is concerned. I intend to have a little chat with him this weekend."

Oh, God! She visibly swallowed. What had Robbie done now? "Please take it easy with him, Boyd." The minute she said it, she realised she had betrayed her own anxieties.

"Surely I never come down *too* hard on him?" Boyd asked, hardening his heart against the meltingly lovely *pleading* image she presented. It was high time to pull Robbie up, before he totally ran off the rails. He had received information that Robbie had been getting in over his head, gambling. He was even doing business with a very unsavoury character, suspected of money laundering. That had to cease.

"I thought we'd ride out towards Mount Garnet," he said, briskly changing the subject. "You've brought some riding gear, haven't you?" If not, he knew she kept clothes at the house.

She had hardly been listening, wondering exactly what he had learned about Robbie. The gambling, of course. The drugs? What else? Robbie could be wonderfully sweet—at least with her—but he wasn't as yet a really strong character. Nothing got past Boyd.

"You're trembling," he said, suddenly putting a strong hand on her bare arm, his thumb moving almost caressingly over the silky skin.

Instantly heat raged around her body. Her skin was melting as the hot blood fizzed through her arteries, ensuring she shook even further. "Yes, I will come riding with you. I was just trying to remember the last time we went riding alone," she managed, hoping she hadn't turned scarlet. Both of them had been riding since they could walk. Both of them were very accomplished. Heavens, Boyd was a top class polo player. But she couldn't remember the last time they had been on their own.

He laughed, sounding particularly at ease, even happy.

It came to her how much she loved his voice and his laugh! It was a sound she adored, yet somehow it disturbed her. It made her bones turn liquid. Even the way he said her name was enough to turn her knees to jelly.

"I'm surprised you don't remember," he said, suddenly pinning her with his blue eyes. "You told me you hated me and I couldn't placate you."

Didn't he realise it had just been another outburst against the pull she felt towards him? She willed herself to speak calmly. "I don't hate you, Boyd. It's just sometimes I'm not at ease with you. Or you with me. I'm not a fool."

How could she possibly say: *You're the moon and stars to me. When you touch me I dissolve?*

Why did she become so erotically charged with Boyd and no one else?

He was looking at her intently. "I realise I make you sparkle with temper, revolt, whatever. I have a mental image of you at the age it all started. You were around sixteen. You'd been really sweet up until then."

You mean I was your little slave.

"It's called growing up," she said coolly. "Finding one's own identity. Sometimes you do make me very angry," she admitted. "You're so terribly…"

"What?" He pressed for an answer.

"Dominant," she flashed back with spirit. "The family idol, born to be worshipped. You mock me like I'm a—"

"Nonsense!" he cut in. "Why are you so unwilling to really answer my question? It's all evasion with you these days. That makes me sad. It's not any authority I might have that angers you. It's something else. So far as the mockery goes, it's the other way around. I see it in your face and in your voice. I can see it *now*." His eyes swept over her, marking the tension in her body, which looked so entrancingly fragile but he knew was in fact quite athletic.

"Boyd, everyone is watching us," she whispered a warning, her nerves exquisitely frayed.

"That's okay," he answered without concern. "They're well used to the friction between us by now."

"How can you call me evasive, Boyd? Did I not just agree to go riding with you?" she asked, pleased to have tripped him up. Then it struck her. "We *are* going on our own, aren't we, or are you getting up a party?"

"A party of *two*, Leona," he told her dryly. "I'm after your company *alone*. No need to bring in the rest of the family."

"Right!" She tilted her chin as she prepared to move off.

"You used to love me," he said, very, very gently to her averted profile.

It stopped her in her tracks. It was still so deliriously *true*.

She moved back to him in that moment, wanting to throw herself at him, clamp her arms around him. Never let go. Have his arms move to embrace her. If he kissed her she feared she might lose consciousness. Or maybe her soul would float out of her body into his. Instead, she raised herself on tiptoe to be nearer to that so dear yet so dangerous face. "I don't any more," she said.

There was safety in deception. Much better to be safe than horribly sorry.

For well over an hour they rode through a countryside that had never seemed so luminous to her. Along the eastern seaboard and even deep into the Outback the land had received wonderful life-giving rain and overnight the land had renewed itself. The light beneath the caverns of trees was jewelled, the display of blossom sumptuous, the air sweet with a hundred different haunting perfumes. Riding together so companionably was too precious to be described. Leona wanted to retain the memory for ever. The sight of him, the familiarity and the exciting *strangeness,* the profile she loved, that clean cut chiselled jaw. With his head half turned away one would have assumed his eyes would be very dark to match the black of his hair and his strongly marked brows. They were anything but—sometimes his eyes were so blue they looked violet. He really was a dream come true.

* * *

Out of the golden glare of the sunlight and down into the dappled green sanctuary of one of the many creeks that wound their way across the estate, he turned his head to smile lazily at her. His eyes, even in the shade, blazed. His wide-brimmed hat, a soft grey, was tilted at a rakish angle. Riding gear suited him wonderfully well. "Enjoying yourself?" he asked.

"I love it!" Leona responded with uncomplicated joy. "I especially love water. All the time we've been riding we've been in sight and sound of it."

"That's what's so powerfully attractive about the estate." He studied her smiling open face with pleasure. "You don't feel threatened by me when you're on horseback?"

"I'm secure in the knowledge I could gallop away from you." She laughed, one hand lightly holding the reins of her pure Arabian mare, as nimble and sure-footed as ever a mare could be. "Anyway, you've never really done anything to threaten me," she added.

"I think I have," he answered slowly.

The way he said it shook her to the marrow. She had to look away. Curly tendrils of her hair had escaped from her ponytail, glowing brightly against the cream of her skin. "You sound as though you care." She couldn't help the revealing tinge of sadness in her voice.

"Of course I do," he answered, almost roughly.

"Good!" she retorted, suddenly very tense. In fact she was starting to feel light-headed. "At least you know with *me* you can't have it all your own way."

"You think I do?" He leaned forward to caress the bay's neck.

"You're quite daunting in a way, you know."

"Leo, that's absolute nonsense," he said crisply.

Her breath fluttered. "No." She could feel the heat in her cheeks. She even felt like bursting into tears, he moved her so unbearably. That alone gave him a power she could never match.

"Then tell me," he demanded. "In what way?"

"In *every* way!" she said a little wildly. "Don't let it bother you. You can't help being like that." Despite the lovely cool of the creek, she could feel trickles of sweat run between her breasts. She had to stop this conversation before her emotions got right out of hand. That would be a very serious mistake.

"Maybe it's proved a pretty effective defence," he suggested, as though he had discovered the answer. His handsome, dynamic face was caught in a shaft of sunlight. She realised he looked unexpectedly serious, faintly troubled.

"Against what?" Horribly, her voice wobbled.

He turned a concentrated gaze to her. "Do you remember when you were a little kid you used to pester me with questions?"

"The miracle is you used to answer me." Despite

herself, she gave him her lovely smile, her green eyes changing from stormy to dancing.

"You had such an insatiable curiosity about everything. You read so widely, even as a child."

"That may have been because I was so lonely after my mother died. You know, sometimes when I'm walking about the lake, I hear her calling to me," she confided with a poignant little air.

That didn't surprise him. Many times he had fancied he had seen his own mother near the little stone temple that stood beside a secluded part of the lake. "We never lose the images of those we love," he murmured gently, wanting only to comfort her.

"She was a beautiful woman, Aunt Alexa. She was so kind to me." She sighed deeply, in many ways still the child denied her beloved mother. "After my mother died—the way she was killed— I thought I'd never get on my pony again. *You* were the one who helped me through that. Not my father. He was too dazed. He went off to some distant planet. It was *you* who convinced me it was what my mother would have wanted. She loved horses. She adored riding. You made me understand that although peril can be anywhere, we have to go on with our lives; we have to hold our simple pleasures close."

"Then I was good for something," he said, a faint twist to his sculpted mouth.

"You were. You *are*," she said, unbearably conscious of his closeness and the fact that they were alone together. But did it really have to put her in such a frenzy? Why, for the love of God, couldn't she relax? Was it because she knew Boyd, heir to the Blanchard fortune, would always be denied her? Maybe she had to accept, once and for all, that he was much too much for her.

The silence between them had taken on a deeply intimate turn whether she wanted it or not. She had the strongest notion that the nerve fibres in their bodies were reaching out to draw them together. When all was said and done, he knew her better than anyone. Her eyes smarted with tears. To be together like this always. To have their relationship develop and flourish as she wanted.

She knew in her heart that it wasn't possible. It wouldn't be allowed. That was the reason she kept that side of her hidden. Now alarm bells were going off in her head. How easy it was to slip into a dream. But it wouldn't do at all. Boyd was so far above her she couldn't begin to calculate the distance. Resolutely she squared her shoulders. "D'you want a race? Let's say to the old ruin?" she challenged him. The old ruin was what they called an extraordinary rocky outcrop on a wilder part of the estate.

"Flower Face, you couldn't beat me," he answered, slowly coming out of his elegant slouch.

"Then I'm going to have a darn good try." Abruptly she turned the mare, spurring her into action. They were tearing up the fairly sharp incline, vanishing down the other side while startled magpies croaked their high displeasure and wild doves shot up into the blue, blue air.

He was giving her a start. She knew that, not sure if in plunging away she wasn't revealing what an emotional coward she was. What made her so emotionally insecure? Was it because she had lost her mother at such a tender age? In many ways she had lost her father to his grief. Lord knew Delia hadn't turned out to be a mother substitute. She couldn't even mother her own son. Galloping wasn't half as dangerous as getting into an intimate conversation with Boyd.

She travelled so fast towards the ruins that an old time Western movie posse might have been giving chase. She wondered excitedly when he was going to close in on her.

To her left was a thick copse of cottonwoods, the golden poplars whose foliage put on such a wonderful brilliant yellow display in the autumn; to her right Chinese elms covered in spring's delicate whiteish-green samaras. Beyond that an indigenous forest of eucalypts in a country where the gum tree was king.

Did anyone who didn't ride realise the wonderful exhilaration of being in the saddle? Her breasts beneath her cream silk shirt rose and fell with her exertions. The balls of her feet, encased in expensive riding boots felt weightless in the stirrups. Compared to the order of the rest of the estate, she was heading into near virgin country as she veered off to take the short cut to the ruins.

She sucked in her breath as the remaining section of an ancient weathered wall threw up a challenge. The wall was covered in an apple-green vine with a beautiful mauve trumpet flower. It would be a very small risk taking the wall. The mare was a good jumper; she rarely stumbled, never baulked. Leona felt completely safe. She had taken far higher obstacles than this. Taking obstacles had claimed her mother's life, but everyone had agreed it was a freak accident, not a miscalculation on her mother's part. Leona trusted to her own judgement.

They literally sailed over the wall. She gave a great shout of triumph, even though her breath had shortened and her breasts were heaving. The old ruins were dead ahead. They looked for all the world like tumbled stone masonry and pillars. She knew she could beat him. What a thrill! She absolutely revelled in the thought.

When Boyd realised she was about to jump the old weathered wall his heart gave a great leap like a salmon making upstream. He wasn't sure, but he thought he shouted, "No!" In an instant he was back in time, caught up in a terrible moment of *déjà vu*. Reining the bay in sharply, he sat stock still in the saddle, back erect, but driven into shutting his eyes. Nothing ever really healed. For a moment he was a boy of fourteen again, waiting for Serena to return so they could all go swimming. He didn't think he could bear to suffer a *worse* loss. He had a vision of Serena's body, brought back to the house on a stretcher. The sorrow he had seen. His mother, Alexa, her beautiful face distorted by grief; the pulverising shock and grief of the others. Leona's father had been unable to speak, totally gutted. Rupert had taken charge of everything, as was his way, his strong autocratic features set in stone.

He opened his eyes again as he heard Leona's shout of victory. She was galloping hell for leather towards the ruins. Like her mother, she brimmed over with life. He was over his fear now, but for several moments he sat on his quivering horse, trying to quell the sudden upsurge of anger that swept in to take the place of his enormous relief.

"Sorry, Boyd, *dear*, I beat you!" She waved an arm high above her head and, not content with that, pulled off her wide brimmed hat and threw it rapturously in the air, bringing home her victory.

"Goodness, you're not mad, are you?" she asked in the very next second, catching sight of the bright sharp anger in his face. He had dismounted, too, and was stalking towards her.

"Why do you take risks?" he gritted with what she took to be hostility.

"I don't. I never do." Hurriedly she tried to defend herself. "Risks? Don't be absurd." This was Boyd. How could she be afraid of him? Boyd would never hurt her. "You're upset," she said as she quickly comprehended. "There's no need to be. I wouldn't do anything stupid."

His eyes burned with the blue intensity of sapphires. "Your mother didn't do anything stupid."

Now both of them were confronting the past. She remembered the horror everyone had felt on that tragic day. The utter disbelief that life, as they had known it, was for ever changed. Her father had been near catatonic. The tears had poured out of Aunt Alexa's eyes. Geraldine had had her arms around her, trying to comfort a loved child. A Blanchard uncle was there with a second wife. That marriage hadn't lasted either. She remembered the way she had afterwards clung to Boyd like some little monkey too scared to let go.

Now she tried desperately to offer conciliation. "We've had a lovely ride. Please don't spoil it."

"Spoil it?" He knew he was losing control, something that never happened. "What you had to do was *not* tackle that damned wall. It could have cost you your neck."

Would anything go as she hoped? Temper flashed. "What I did," she told him defiantly, "was jump a fairly low obstacle. I've jumped a lot higher than that."

"Not on *that* little mare you haven't," he said with a vigorous jerk of his head towards the pure bred Arabian.

She stared back at him in disbelief, forgetting all caution, missing the fear behind his grimness. "So she isn't the tallest horse in the stable, but I love her. In any case she's sure-footed. Who the devil do you think you are, telling me what I can and cannot do?" she demanded. "Who are you to rule my life? No wonder I resent you. No wonder I've fought you for years. No wonder—"

She was on such a roll she was completely unprepared for his explosive reaction. Sparks seemed to be flowing from him like tiny glittering stars. While the blood rushed in her ears, he pulled her to him in a kind of fury, locking one steely arm around her, his left hand thrusting up her chin. "Oh, shut up bleating about your resentments and irritations," he bit off with unfamiliar violence. "You irritate the hell out of me."

He had confirmed it at long last. She let out a cry of pain. "I was wondering when you'd get around to admitting it," she said, small white teeth clenched. They were standing so close together all her senses were reeling. Her blood ran blisteringly hot in her veins. To her distress she knew she couldn't handle this. She was shaking with the effort to hold herself together. Dazzling sunlight spun around them like an impenetrable golden web.

"Let me *go*, you savage!" Even as the words left her lips she was shocked that she had said it. Boyd, a savage! Why couldn't she shout, *I love you*? Why did she for ever have to hold it in? It was agony. There was no hope of getting free unless he released her.

"Count yourself lucky I'm not!" He laughed, but that didn't lessen the bright anger on his face. "I'm not going to let you go, Leona, until I've taught you a necessary lesson. No point in struggling. I've been far too indulgent with you, taking all the little taunts you throw at me on a regular basis. Just how long do I have to wait before you call a ceasefire?"

How could she possibly demolish the defensive structure she had so painstakingly built up in a matter of moments? "For ever!" she shouted fiercely, not fully realising how wildly provocative she had become.

And that sealed her fate.

With a face like thunder Boyd lowered his head. He hauled her right up against him, her delicate body near breakable in his grip, intent on finding her beautiful, softly textured mouth. He felt capable of something monstrous, like picking her up and carrying her off into the forest like some primitive caveman. Sometimes she literally drove him crazy.

The impact on Leona was equally tremendous. Yet hadn't she always known that something like this would happen? This was the man she loved. And, from time to time, *hated*. Because he made her feel so…so what? Off her brain? She couldn't move. Her riding clothes seemed to have turned to gossamer. She had to tense her body so it wouldn't dissolve into his. She had never experienced such tumultuous emotions in her whole life. It was seismic.

His long fingers plunged into her hair, catching up handfuls of red-gold curls. "I get so tired of your fighting me," he groaned.

Her legs had given way to the extent that she thought if he hadn't been holding her so powerfully she would have slid down his body to crumple at his feet. "Open your mouth," he said. "I want to taste you."

The sensuality of the moment was ferocious. It stole her breath. Desperately she clamped her lips together. The utter senselessness of it. His tongue prised them apart. "This is something else you can resent," he told her harshly.

To save herself from going totally under, like a

swimmer in wild surf, she closed her eyes and let the giant waves of emotion engulf her.

He was kissing her, devouring her, eating her, as if her mouth were a peach. To make it worse, she was so driven by sensation she began to eat him. It certainly felt like it. All she knew was desire. It was terrifying. So sensuous, so *natural*, so voluptuous, so God-given. To ease the strength of his hold on her, she thrust one of her legs between his, making her acutely aware that he was powerfully aroused. And *she* was the cause of it.

When he let go of her—all but pushed her away—she felt so disorientated, so weak-limbed, she actually fell down into the thick, honey-coloured grasses that grew in a wide circle around the ruins. "I don't believe you just did that," she said eventually, her hands pressed to her temples as if they were pounding.

"It happened all right." Forcefully, Boyd drew air into his lungs.

"I hated it," she said. An outrageous piece of lying. And it wouldn't help her.

"Don't lie to me, Leo," he chided her curtly. "It won't work." He gave them both a necessary minute of respite, then he reached down to pull her to her feet, keeping a hold on her swaying figure.

Her green eyes met his, huge with shock. "But I *need* to lie to you." The truth would involve love and *love* was a fatal word. "Don't you understand? We're *cousins*. *Family*."

He gave a jagged laugh. "Second cousins, more or less. Less, actually, when you consider your grandfather and my great-uncle were half-brothers."

"Does that make a difference?" How could she possibly steal Boyd away from the family? She knew Rupert fervently wished for an alliance between him and Chloe Compton, who was an heiress in her own right. How could she challenge powerful, menacing Rupert? She would never be allowed to walk away from that one.

"A difference to what?" Boyd rasped, uncaring of his father's plans, his own man.

"You mean you were doing me a great *honour* kissing me?" She felt unendurably pressured, not even sure what she was saying. Whether indeed she was making any sense.

"I didn't think for one moment you'd admit to a passionate response," he said bitterly.

How was she managing to hide all her yearning? She was a woman, flesh and blood, not a pillar of ice. But she *was* managing. She saw it in his eyes.

He was waiting for something from her—something important—only she was in such a state of high arousal she didn't know how best to answer. She didn't know how best to handle a situation she herself had created. Instead, she concentrated fiercely on a distant copse of trees. "Let's set the record straight. That was an *angry* response, more or less." Anger was safe. It was what he was used to from her, after all.

His expression became hard and mocking. "That's it! Do another runner." His brilliant blue eyes darkened to cobalt.

"And just who am I supposed to be running away from?" Unable to help herself, she took the bait.

"Hell, Leo, we both know that."

How she felt the power of those blazing eyes. She was shaking all over, engulfed by raging passions.

"Oh, for God's sake!" Boyd, contemplating her extreme agitation, suddenly relented. He reached out and drew her against his chest as if she were still a child, allowing her to stand until she was quiet within the half circle of his arms.

"Here, let's get you home," he murmured, somehow preventing his hands from sliding all over her perfect body. A body he wanted to cover like a man sought to cover the body of the woman he desired.

To Leona's ears, he sounded near defeated. That was *so* unlike Boyd—but he kept a supportive arm around her. It was a measure of his very real affection for her, she thought gratefully. Affection was allowed. The family would allow affection.

Boyd must have been on the same wavelength

because he asked in a very dry voice, "Anyone for a cup of tea?"

She fell into line. "I don't drink tea."

"Neither do I."

"I know." She dared to look up at him, seeking some measure of reassurance. "Was kissing me a game?" If he said yes, she thought she might die.

"If it was a game, it's one I'm not sure I know the rules to," he said grimly.

"Sometimes I'm afraid, Boyd." She tried to explain herself. Without her mother, with a largely "absent" father, she had become used to keeping things in. It was all right to worship Boyd. He was the supernova in the family. She was part of the clan certainly, but still fairly low in the pecking order. For her and Boyd to become romantically involved would cause huge problems. She could even lose her job. Would Bea allow it? She badly needed time to consider the magnitude of what had just happened. Both of them had responded so passionately they might have been trying to make up for lost time. Would the force grow, the desperation?

"Poor baby!" Boyd murmured, as though all too aware of her fears. He was suppressing urges so intense he didn't know how he was able to withstand them. "Come on." He used his normal persuasive voice. "Home." He bent to give her a leg up onto the Arabian mare, who was standing so quietly she might have been listening in on their conversation. Then, when Leona was in the saddle, he turned away to whistle up his bay, who was lightly grazing several feet away.

The secrets of the heart, he thought. It was time to bring a few of them out into the open. His feelings for Leona, the strong bond they had always shared, was stored in his blood.

CHAPTER THREE

"GOSH, THERE YOU ARE! I've been searching for you everywhere." Robbie, looking almost distraught, rushed down the corridor of the west wing towards her. "Been riding?" He glanced down at her clothes.

"You know I love to ride," Leona answered, trying to gauge his mood. "What time did you get here?"

"Oh, about an hour ago," he said. "I had hoped we could have a game of tennis."

"I don't see why not." Leona lifted her wrist and glanced at her watch. It would be daylight for hours yet. Besides, physical exertion might dampen her flaming passions. "Is everything okay?" She stared directly into his dark eyes. Should she warn him that Boyd planned to have a little chat with him? Perhaps not yet.

"It is now." He shrugged cheerfully. "You know I'm lost at Brooklands without you."

"Even so, you seem off balance."

"I'm fine, Leo," he said, now faintly testy. "I had the great misfortune to run—literally—into Tonya. That woman is the very devil. Jinty is in wonderful spirits. She gave me a great big hug. If I didn't know better I'd have thought I was her favourite nephew. Rupe, needless to say, was overjoyed to see me again. Where's Boyd? Never sighted him."

"He came riding with me," Leona said, deliberately offhand though it took a huge effort. She continued on her way down the picture-lined gallery towards her room.

"Did he now!" Robbie exclaimed, following her up. "The relationship growing, is it?"

"Not that I'm aware of." She kept on walking.

"Despite the fact you're Boyd's marmalade kitten?"

She had to laugh at such a fanciful description. "I always thought of myself as the stray duckling."

"Ah, Leo, sweetie, you yearn for his good graces," Robbie said, loudly sighing. "So do I, for that matter. Black tie tonight?"

"You know it is."

"I bet you've brought something exquisite to wear." How beautiful Leo was, Robbie thought proudly. Glorious hair, glorious skin, glorious eyes—a romantic dream.

"Nothing else like it in the world," she joked. In fact she had brought two beautiful evening dresses with her. *You know who for.* "I tell you what. Let me have a quick shower after that gallop. Get into your gear and I'll meet you at the courts in around twenty minutes."

"You're an angel." He hugged her, an inbred Latin style in all his movements. "Shall I ask Simon and his girlfriend to join us? I think Simon is planning on announcing their engagement quite soon." Simon was one of the Blanchard cousins, also working for the firm.

"Good idea. Emma is so nice."

"And her family own a *nice* big sheep station," Robbie pointed out waspishly. "Let's not put that little fact aside."

"Ah, well, money usually marries money," Leona said.

"And power begets power. How enviable it all is! And a very good idea, I suppose. These days women get half of what a guy has if they split up, so why then shouldn't women bring a dowry with them like the old days? Rupe is madly pushing poor old Chloe at Boyd."

"Robbie," Leona reproved too sharply but she couldn't help herself.

"Leona," he responded heavily. "You have to remember there's always tremendous pressure on people with lots of money to keep up. They have *huge* overheads. Houses, cars, planes, yachts, skillions of employees. To old Rupe's eyes it would be utterly right to push Boyd and

Chloe together. She's a nice girl. Bit dim but everyone likes her. Even me and I'm vaguely anti-women. After all, two fortunes are better than one. It's not marrying for money at all. It's plain common sense."

"Then maybe I shouldn't point out that Annalise quite likes you," she put in lightly. Annalise was one of the clan, an intelligent, graceful young woman, still at university.

"Does she really?" Robbie's lean cheeks flushed with colour.

Leona smiled at him.

"I'd never be allowed to court Annalise," he said gloomily. "I'm the peasant in your midst."

"Oh, don't start that phoney inferiority stuff again," she warned him. "It's all a pretence. Even I can see you're an attractive guy. There's no reason why you couldn't ask Annalise out. I'm sure she'd accept."

Robbie, for answer, suddenly vaulted effortlessly over an antique chair, one of several set along the wall. "Have you heard from the parents?" The acid was back in his tone. Leona's father and Delia were currently in London, a mix of business and pleasure. They weren't due back for another fortnight.

"I heard from Dad the other night," Leona volunteered, still concerned by how superficial that brief conversation had been. Her father might have been reading from a prepared script, though maybe he'd felt inhibited by Delia's presence most probably behind him.

Perhaps Leona's great likeness to her mother tied her poor father in knots. Instead of turning to her as all he had left of his beautiful young first wife, he had turned not away, but aside. Leona was certain that her father didn't love Delia. Never had. He had simply felt it necessary as a Blanchard, a man of consequence who moved in high society, to have a partner, a token wife. Delia, a career socialite, was glamorous enough. She could play her part. Without being in the same league as the main family, or occupying the same stage, her father was nonetheless a wealthy man. Delia would never have married a nobody, thus proving Robbie's sage theory.

"Mummy dearest was too busy to ring *me*," Robbie said, as though thrilled to bits that she hadn't.

"She didn't speak to me either, Robbie."

"We're like two lost children, aren't we, Leo? Makes us vulnerable, don't you think?"

A truth that couldn't be ignored. "Well, I don't intend to let it swamp me," she said. "Don't let it swamp you either. It's not easy being part and yet not a part of the mega-rich."

"Well, *you're* in," Robbie said. "You're part of the tribe. I never will be." They had arrived at her door.

"You've got lots going for you, Robbie. Now, go

change. I'll meet you down on the courts. We'll beat those two."

"A piece of cake!" Robbie smiled, returned to good humour.

By the time they came back from their triumphant doubles match the house had its full complement of weekend guests. Pre-dinner drinks in the formal drawing room. Dinner at eight. Leona loved these occasions. She loved seeing the men in black tie. She loved being given the opportunity to dress up. She knew Jinty and the highly ambitious Tonya would be looking their most glamorous. The sisters bore a close family resemblance, both blond and blue-eyed, but whereas Jinty made the most of her eye-catching full figure, Tonya had elected to go for skin and bone. For that matter Leona couldn't actually remember ever seeing Tonya eat anything.

She had wondered why Chloe Compton wasn't among the guests until Geraldine had informed her that Chloe was attending the wedding of an old school friend in Auckland, New Zealand.

"Chloe won't go away. Dearie me, no!" Geraldine offered, somewhat darkly.

"Go away?" What was Gerri going on about?

"Don't be dense, child." Geraldine had actually pinched her. "It doesn't suit you. Every last member of the Compton tribe is campaigning for Chloe to become Mrs. Boyd Blanchard."

"But I thought you *all* were!" Leona answered in amazement. "Let's face it. It's Rupert's dearest wish."

"Bugger Rupert!" said Geraldine.

Bathed, make-up and hair done, Leona looked down at the two evening dresses spread out on her Versailles-style bed. One was a beautifully draped emerald-green georgette silk with a *faux* diamond brooch detail at the waist. Green, after all, was her colour and the dress was definitely sexy. Maybe too sexy. The other was chiffon of a colour that defied description. Neither pink nor apricot but a marvellous blend of the two. Bea had actually picked it out for her.

"This colour was made for you, Leona, my dear, with that magnificent mane of hair. Not many can get away with the ethereal style either, but you can. Take it. It's a gift!"

Closely fitted to the hip, embroidered to one side with matching flowers and leaves, the neckline plunged, as was the fashion, the skirt flowed gracefully to the floor. No doubt about it, it was exquisite. And it looked even better on.

What kind of statement did she wanted to make? The *femme fatale* or the springtime nymph? In the end she opted for the ethereal, romantic look. No getting away from it, it did suit her style of looks and she was rather worried about pushing her sexuality. She couldn't afford to be too obvious about it. *Sweet little Leona* to Rupert—that was the way he would want her to remain. Rupert wouldn't hear of any other woman for his son but Chloe Compton. She understood that fully. And Rupert had long since developed the habit of getting everything he wanted.

But then—Boyd had kissed her. If he never kissed her again, she would remember it for her whole life. And, remembering, live off it. Wasn't there a law that said one was only allowed one great love in life? She hoped not.

When she walked into the drawing room in her high heeled evening sandals, her chiffon skirt floating around her, everyone with one notable exception, looked at her with open pleasure, Peter Blanchard, one of the cousins, with open adoration. She had known Peter all of her life. He had been her escort on many, many occasions and she was very fond of him. He was good-looking, clever and charming in his way. He had a number of university degrees under his belt, one from Harvard Business School. Like most of the clan, he worked for Blanchards.

Unfortunately, he couldn't hold a candle to Boyd, who was staring across the room at her, blue eyes glittering. She started to breathe deeply. That

was right. In and out. She had the sudden deliri-
ous notion that her dress had turned transparent.
Her glance shot away to Rupert, who was smiling
his approval. Rupert was standing with his son in
front of the fireplace, with its white marble
surround and magnificent eighteenth century
English mirror. Both men were of a height, both
possessed of a charisma that commanded attention.

The fireplace when not in use in spring and
summer was generally occupied by a large
Chinese fish bowl filled with masses and masses
of flowers and greenery. Tonight the big blue and
white bowl held a profusion of pink Oriental lilies,
with twisting dried branches, spear grasses and a
fan of palms. Leona noticed abstractedly that the
lilies matched the colours of her dress—pink with
speckled golden-apricot throats.

Geraldine, seated on one of the damask upholstered sofas in conversation with one of the
Blanchard wives, waved her over. She presented a
vision of striking eccentricity in her favourite
imperial purple with diamond and amethyst
earrings as big as chandeliers swinging from her
ears. Tonya was half turned away, as though
Leona's entrance had been staged and in any case
was of no interest to her. Champagne glass in hand,
she looked very glamorous in a short evening gown
of a deep glowing shade of fuchsia. All the women
had made a real effort to sparkle and glow. Simon's

serene Emma wore blue to match her eyes. It was a comparatively modest gown given the evening wear around her, but she wore it with unselfconscious ease, certain of her place in the scheme of things.

And here was Jinty, the hostess with the mostest. That certainly applied tonight. No one, but no one could hope to outshine Jinty, Leona thought as Jinty flowed towards her. She had gone all out tonight. Money simply wasn't an issue. She wore a couture black satin strapless gown, above which her creamy bosom swelled proudly. Her thick blonde hair was coiffed to perfection, swept up and back. She would have a hairdresser in residence. But everything was simply a backdrop to showcase the "Blanchard Diamonds".

They were so glorious that the owner of the most magnificent collection of jewels in the world, the Queen of England might have envied them. The suite comprised three pieces—necklace, pendant earrings and bracelet. All white diamonds, they were colourless and flawless. A double row of pear-shaped diamonds encircled Jinty's neck. Appended to the bottom row was a large square-shaped diamond enhancer enclosing a huge canary diamond that Leona knew weighed in at over thirty carats. The earrings alone featured two nine carat drops that flashed and scintillated with Jinty's every movement. Everyone in the family knew the suite had been acquired at the turn of the twentieth century from a famous South African billionaire who had plenty more where they'd come from. The diamonds had been mined at De Beers, Cecil Rhodes' first diamond mine. So the suite had a history.

The last time Leona had seen the whole suite Aunt Alexa had been wearing it at a grand state ball. Jinty often wore the superb earrings. Sometimes the bracelet. But so far the necklace hadn't had an outing. Tradition had it that the suite was to be handed down through the generations for the use of the current wife of the head of the Blanchard family. Which made Jinty merely a custodian, which was a blessing. If Rupert and Jinty ever split up, her share would be in multiples of millions, but she would never get away with the "Blanchard Diamonds".

"Jinty, you look simply marvelous!" Leona said, because she *did*.

"Why, thank you, dear!" Jinty responded brightly. "The diamonds make me feel like a goddess."

"They look wonderful on you. They really do." And she meant it.

"And you look perfectly beautiful as usual," Jinty responded graciously. "Where did you get that dress? The colour is extraordinary. Especially with your hair."

"Bea picked it out," Leona said.

Jinty gave a faint shudder. "Can't stand the woman, though I know she's a genius of sorts. Ugly though, don't you think? Rupert won't hear a word against her. Now, I must get you a glass of champagne." She turned away in time to see Boyd approaching. "Ah, here's Boyd with one," she said brightly.

Boyd stopped in front of them, handing a glass of champagne to Leona. "No need to tell you you look ravishing, Leona," he said, an unmistakably caressing intonation in his voice.

"That she does," Jinty seconded rather abruptly. "Where's that stepbrother of yours, Leo? We can't go into dinner without him."

"There's plenty of time," Boyd murmured, looking towards the entrance hall. The circular library table that stood in the middle of the spacious hall, which was paved in a diamond pattern of marble and stone, was the perfect spot for another stunning flower arrangement, this time a profusion of roses, gerberas, lisianthus and leaves. "Here he is now," Boyd said as Robbie suddenly hove into view.

"Slowcoach!" Jinty spoke crisply, a little afraid of Robbie's satirical tongue. She didn't linger, but moved off as though her husband had beckoned. He hadn't.

Leona stood with the fragile crystal wineglass in her hand.

"Come and sit down," Boyd said.

"Geraldine was looking out for me."

"Geraldine can have her moment later. You're mine now." His hand slipped beneath her elbow. Maybe she was becoming paranoid, but she had a sense that the whole room had snapped to attention. Tonya of the high slanting cheekbones was looking daggers at her. Tonya was having a lot of difficulty accepting Boyd was as good as spoken for. Ignoring the competition, especially in the form of Chloe Compton, was a heroic effort or a piece of madness on Tonya's part so far as Leona was concerned, but Tonya had thrown herself wholeheartedly into the hunt.

Maybe all we women are delusional, Leona thought. Seeing signs and intentions where there were none.

Robbie, looking gratifyingly handsome and very Italian in his formal gear, which any discerning eye could see *was* Italian and a perfect fit, met up with them in the centre of the drawing room with its apple-green and gold upholstery and curtains and a splendid duck-egg blue, white and gold plated ceiling.

"Sorry I'm late," he apologised. "Usually I don't have a problem, but I had trouble with my tie. You look wonderful, Leo." His dark eyes moved over her with pride and admiration. "Doesn't she, Boyd?" he queried, not so artlessly.

Boyd just smiled. "I don't know if wonderful quite says it, Robbie. Magical comes to mind."

Robbie suddenly caught sight of Jinty. "Good grief!" he breathed. "What's she got on, the Crown Jewels?"

"Those, my man, are the Blanchard Diamonds," Boyd corrected him. "Not the same thing."

"You've seen the earrings before," Leona reminded him. "Jinty often wears them."

"But the necklace!" Robbie was looking dazzled. "I've an overwhelming desire to go over and take a closer look, but I don't know what would happen. Our Jinty has a mean streak. She might punch me in the nose. I have to say those diamonds look great on her, but think what they would look like on *you*, Leo!" He turned to her.

"No, no, no!" Leona shook her head vigorously, making the deep waves and curls dance. The Blanchard Diamonds were destined for Boyd's *wife*. She wasn't wearing a necklace anyway. She had nothing that could remotely match the jewellery around her in any case. But she was wearing her mother's lovely earrings, a daisy wheel of pink sapphires and tiny diamonds with a silver baroque pearl appended from each.

"A Midsummer Night's Dream!" Boyd suggested. "You don't need diamonds, Leo. A crown of flowers on your head would be perfect."

Robbie stared up at the taller man. "That's it

exactly. God, you're a romantic guy, Boyd. No wonder the women love you. You say really romantic things."

"To Leona, I think you mean?" Boyd's voice was vaguely self-mocking.

Robbie was still staring back at Boyd thoughtfully. "Come to think of it, yes. To Leona." He made a sudden move. "Listen, I'm going to grab a Martini."

"As long as you don't make it bath-sized," Boyd warned. Some time tomorrow morning he intended to have his little talk with Robbie. He would not be allowed to continue on the path he'd been taking.

By eight o'clock everyone was seated at the long mahogany table. Twenty-four in all, looking as though they belonged perfectly in such a grand room. It was Jinty's job to keep an excellent table. Rupert expected it of her, so she had made it her business to employ the best people. Older members of the clan, however, had privately expressed the opinion that occasionally Jinty's food was too exotic for their taste.

Leona had been placed beside Peter, a little right of centre table. Robbie was opposite her. Geraldine was to her brother's right. Boyd was seated to Jinty's right with Tonya all but opposite him. Everyone was arranged according to the pecking order.

"Some artistic genius has arranged the flowers," Leona remarked to Peter, touching a gentle finger to a rose petal.

"Can't be Jinty." He bent closer to whisper in her ear. "Some of darling Jinty's early floral arrangements went spectacularly wrong."

Strangely, it was true. Leona had previously thought one could scarcely go wrong with beautiful flowers but obviously there were many routes to getting things right. There was definitely an art to mixing colours. Tonight, tall glass cylinder vases wrapped in ivy, equally spaced down the table, held an exquisite mix of yellow and cream roses and buttercup-coloured day lilies. No doubt the flowers had been chosen to complement the cream damask cloth, the gold and white plates and the gold napkin rings. It all looked very lovely.

The first course was served. Superb large white scallops on an Asian risotto cake with fresh pesto and lime slices. That went down well. Sipping at her crisp white wine, which had a tang of citrus to it, Leona caught Boyd's eye. Instantly she experienced an electric touch to her mind, heart and body. How easy it was to become lost in that profoundly blue gaze.

Peter was saying something to her, but she barely heard.

"Are you listening to me?" Peter tapped the knuckles of her hand for attention.

"Of course I am." She had to gather herself. "You were talking about your trip to Antarctica. How it changed you for ever."

Peter smiled, pleased she had been paying attention. The whole family knew he had a real thing for Leona. It was as though he couldn't get past her. "It's an amazing place. A world of blinding white ice. It might sound strange, but there's only one other place in the world where I've been so overwhelmed."

"Our Outback," Leona guessed. "The vastness, the mystical quality, the extraordinary isolation?"

"Very good." Peter tapped her hand again. "Both places have had a powerful effect on me. Sometimes I think I would have liked to be an adventurer," he confided, giving her his endearing smile.

"Instead you're inordinately clever at handling a great deal of money, Peter."

"Well, there's something in that. Can't wait for the polo match tomorrow afternoon. That's what I need, a damned good gallop. You're going to be on the sidelines cheering me on?"

"Wouldn't miss it for the world," she said, smiling.

The main course arrived. Nothing too complicated, more a classic. Racks of spring lamb with a buttery, crisp green herb crust served with a medley of vegetables including freshly baked young courgettes stuffed with peas and spring onions.

Conversation around the table flourished. These country weekends had become something of a ritual. Down the opposite end of the table, their hostess, Jinty, kept talking to Boyd, obviously captivated by his conversation. It was obvious to them all that she was fascinated by her stepson and oblivious to the building tension in her sister, Tonya. Looking at Tonya's strained, impatient face, Leona could feel the turbulent current from where she was sitting. Robbie, across the table, kept catching her eye, his dark eyes glistening with malicious humour. She could read what he was telling her. What did Rupe think about his wife paying so much attention to his son? Rupert, as sharp as they came, would have been observing what was going on. An intolerant man at the best of times, Rupert might have a few words to say to Jinty when the evening was over. He would know Boyd was simply being Boyd, a brilliant conversationalist who, without any effort on his part, became the object of women's fantasies.

Desserts arrived. A choice between a bitter chocolate mousse tart and Rupert's great favourite, a richly flavoured deep-dish apple pie served with double cream.

"I hope Rupert doesn't make a habit of ordering

up that apple pie," Peter murmured. "There has to be an incredible number of calories in it and just look at how much extra cream he's putting on!"

"Don't worry, Rupert will live for ever," Leona murmured back, thinking mournfully that only the good died young.

After a lingering coffee and liqueurs everyone adjourned to the drawing room, where Jinty was to entertain them. Jinty was quite an accomplished *chanteuse*, using her mellow *mezzo* to sing everlasting blues favourites made famous by the likes of Ella Fitzgerald and Peggy Lee. To top it off, she accompanied herself on the big Steinway concert grand.

"Don't clap too much," Peter, who wasn't a music lover, warned Leona in a quick aside, "or we might be here until four in the morning."

As it was, Jinty knew the perfect moment to stop. The entertainment had gone on for the best part of an hour. Now a genuine round of applause broke out when she rose, tall and voluptuous from the piano seat, her somewhat haughty face softened by such appreciation. She gave a little bow, the lights from the four matching giltwood chandeliers as nothing compared to the dazzling white flashes given off by the "Blanchard Diamonds".

"I'd give my soul for the earrings alone," one of the Blanchard wives was heard to whisper to her husband, perhaps as an incentive for him to work harder.

Leona felt she knew better than that. The soul was sacred. Bad enough to give your heart away.

Boyd was much in demand. So much so it was difficult to get near him. Even Tonya's all out efforts at seduction were being sabotaged. One of the great-uncles, a distinguished High Court judge had detained Peter who, though desperate to get back to Leona's side, was compelled to pay his respects.

It was a beautiful evening, the great coffered dome of the sky awesome with stars. Some of the guests had begun to step outside for a breath of garden-fragrant air and to cool the overflow of emotions induced by Jinty's scintillating performance. Turning her head, Leona just chanced to see Jinty quietly remove her diamond pendant earrings—which must have been quite heavy— and slip them into a Limoges ormolu mounted covered bowl, one of a collection on a small circular table that was supported by two gilded swans, their long elegant necks bent.

Now that was careless. Reckless, even. It would be a disaster if any part of the suite went missing. Clearly Jinty trusted everyone, guests and servants alike. Not that Leona didn't, but still… She couldn't in a million years have done it, was amazed that Jinty had. She couldn't begin to imagine Rupert's wrath if the earrings disappeared.

Not that anyone foolish enough to attempt such a criminal act could hope to sell them on the open market. In their own way, the "Blanchard Diamonds" were famous.

Right away she headed towards Jinty to what… remonstrate with her hostess…issue a warning? Jinty wouldn't take kindly to that; married to Rupert Blanchard, she was queen of all she surveyed. Nonetheless Leona was halfway across the room, chiffon skirt flowing, a springtime nymph in flight, when a black-jacketed arm reached for her.

"What's the hurry?"

Excitement surged. She spun to face him. "I was just going to…going to…"

"Get it out, Flower Face," he urged.

What could she possibly say? Jinty has taken off the diamond earrings and left them in a Limoges porcelain bowl back there. Surely an unsafe place? It struck her forcibly that Jinty wouldn't want Boyd to know that. The diamond suite, after all, would one day be handed down to Boyd's wife.

"I was just going for a breath of air," she managed, realising that Jinty needed protection.

"You mean you were going into hiding from Peter," Boyd suggested dryly. "You really should put poor old Pete out of his misery."

"I've never put him *in* his misery," she said sharply. "I can't help it if Peter's got a bit of a crush on me."

"Bit old for a crush, isn't he?" Boyd offered in a sardonic tone of voice. "Peter must be twenty-eight."

"So?" She stared defiantly into his brilliant eyes. "Haven't you heard of men having crushes in their eighties? There was Goethe for one. Tolstoy, I'm sure. Great-Uncle William fell for that twenty-year-old ballet dancer, remember? People in their nineties find their one true love in nursing homes. There must be plenty of others."

"Please, that's more than enough," Boyd said, drawing her to his side. "Don't let's have a brawl here. I've been praying we'd get a moment alone."

"Praying?" The familiar banter had resumed. "I didn't think you liked me all that much."

"But I do enjoy kissing you," he said, sweeping her out onto the terrace. "Where did you learn to be so darn good, by the way?"

"It's called doing what comes naturally." Leona smiled and waggled her fingers at Geraldine, who was standing with a little group of her closest family allies. Geraldine waggled her fingers back, her grey eyes sparking with interest.

"Then you were born an expert."

"So were you." There wasn't time to add anything further.

"Quick, over here," Boyd said, almost lifting her off her feet.

"Whoa!" She blinked, wondering what had happened, then it clicked. "Ah, you've spotted

Tonya." She didn't bother to stifle her impish glee. "Or could it have been Jinty. She's *awfully* fond of you."

He was steering her down a camellia-lined path, walking fast. "I wish she'd remember she's a happily married woman," he said, as though it bothered him.

"That doesn't make her immune to your appeal," she mocked. "And *is* she so happy?"

They were sliding like shadows away from the broad circle of exterior lights and into the mysterious glimmering light beneath the canopy of trees. "Jinty treasures money," he said.

"So do most people," Leona added dryly. "They say they don't, but they do."

"Only Dad is in a position to be far more generous than most men. Money matters a great deal to women like Jinty."

"So when Rupert says *jump*, Jinty has to jump." Leona didn't like the idea of jumping on demand.

"I guess that was the deal," Boyd said, his tone dry as ash.

"Does it always have to be deals where there's money?" she asked. "Shouldn't love be stronger than any deal?"

"I'd like to think so," Boyd said.

"Good thing you're your own man then," she mocked him. "Rupert has Chloe lined up for you."

"Think I need you to tell me that?" He glanced down at her, this ravishing young creature who lived to cross swords with him. "This time Dad's wishes and his judgement are way off kilter. I like Chloe. That's a long way from falling in love."

"My thoughts entirely. But she *loves* you," Leona felt obliged to point out. "Listen, can you slow down? Those long legs of yours!"

"Sure," he responded immediately. "Leo, I'm not about to offer Chloe Compton an engagement ring, if that's what you're thinking."

"It surely doesn't matter what *I* think," she said. "I'm only your cousin. Of sorts. Way down the pecking order. About three would you say on a scale of one to ten? If you did want to please your dad and offer Chloe an engagement ring, Tonya might well have a nervous breakdown. It wouldn't be a pretty sight. Not to mention all your exes. Thought of that?"

"I'd be so pleased if you didn't mention my exes," he said. "Which does not include Tonya, by the way. Dad invites her just to annoy me."

"I'm so glad you see that," she said cheerfully. "But you have established quite a reputation as a ladies' man."

He brought them to a halt. "Stop, Leo," he said. "I thought this afternoon might have been lesson enough for you."

She turned up an innocent face. "This afternoon? I don't recall."

"Then let's give you a reminder."

In the second or so it took him to pull her into his arms Leona felt such a concentration of sensation—excitement, rippling desire, a meltdown in her limbs—it was almost terror. Boyd had the power to turn her inside out. Should she trust such power? Should any woman trust such power? And it wasn't just blind sexual yearning. It was much, much more. Like salvation. Or finding her true home.

His soul. Her soul. One and the same. Or had they in kissing opened a door that should never have been opened? Only time would tell.

His hand was lightly around her throat, his thumb gently stroking her chin up to him.

"I want you," he said, scarcely above a murmur.

She tried to speak and found she couldn't. Instead, she gave a convulsive shudder. Fear or longing or a mixture of both? Common sense told her she should pull away. This was Boyd, the Blanchard heir. Out of her league.

"This is madness!"

"Then I've been mad a long time," he said, his mouth trailing kisses all over her face.

Such an admission from Boyd made her forget everything. All sense of caution was in shreds.

His hand moved to her breast, trapped a nipple that had already blossomed.

It took time for cold reason to kick in. *Want?* It had all shades of meaning. Did Boyd want an affair? Did he want to solve the mystery he thought she was? It was a huge open question.

"Boyd, we must stop. This isn't possible…" she gasped.

His voice sounded fathoms deep in languor. "I don't think you really mean that. Anyway, it's happening." Very slowly, as though savouring the ecstasy of the moment, his mouth made its sure return to hers.

Her defences crumbled. Desire over reason. She couldn't resist it. He kissed her and kissed her. And she let him.

She was his. How could she now be deprived of him?

CHAPTER FOUR

TONYA DISCOVERED THEM returning to the house. "Where have you two been?" she called, her tone shrill and demanding.

Boyd laughed. "Tonya, what does it have to do with you?"

The darkness hid Tonya's flush. Even she couldn't miss the lick of sarcasm. "For heaven's sake, Boyd, everyone was wondering where you were, that's all."

"I have enough of the family on my back when I'm at work," Boyd responded, the arm Leona was holding tensing to steel.

"The fact remains that everyone wants to say goodnight." Tonya aimed a glance so fierce at Leona that her eyes glowed in the semi-dark. "Peter has been looking for you everywhere."

"Come on, Tonya," Boyd intervened. "Leona and Peter aren't a couple."

"You'd better tell *him* that," Tonya retorted with a knowing laugh.

"Tonya, why is it you get such an amazing number of things wrong?" Boyd wasn't trying to hide his irritation.

Instinctively Leona pressed her fingers into his jacketed arm, trying to soak up some of his flaring temper. Was Tonya a complete fool?

"I have the evidence of my own eyes." Foolishly, Tonya failed to see what was so obvious to Leona. She was making him angry.

"Then make a wish for a pair of glasses," he retorted curtly.

"Look, why don't we continue on to the house?" Leona made the hasty suggestion, wondering if she had a skerrick of lipstick left. Tonya would fasten onto that in a flash. God knew what questions would be asked then. Tonya obviously needed no encouragement to interfere in other people's business.

"If you were a good sister you would have seen to your brother," she said, rounding on Leona as if she were a recalcitrant schoolgirl. "He says the most impertinent things." Tonya's voice was filled with resentment. "It's difficult to stand there and take it."

"Robbie is given to speaking plainly," Boyd said. "One wonders why you wanted to come this weekend." His voice had taken on a note that would have alerted the thickest skinned woman.

Leona couldn't bear to see Tonya crushed, no matter how well merited the put-down. "Excuse me, won't you?" She broke away. She felt she had little option. They had nearly reached the terrace, which was now almost deserted. If Tonya continued in a similar vein she would surely come to grief. Why was Tonya investing all her energies into trying to attract Boyd? Maybe she was mad after all.

"Where did you get to?" Peter was hovering just inside the French windows, obviously on the lookout for her.

"Were you worried?" Leona asked. Perhaps she should have filled out a logbook. Once she had said her goodnights to a downcast Peter and the rest of the party, Robbie moved swiftly towards her. For a handsome young man he looked ghastly. He was very pale beneath his suntanned skin, his lustrous dark eyes glittering like coals. Obviously he'd had too much to drink. Robbie always did go over the top.

"Where did you go?"

Leona had to fight for control. "You're the third person to ask me that. Or, in Tonya's case, *demanded* to know." Because she loved her stepbrother, she weakened, linking her arm through his, urging him towards the staircase.

"God, she's a stupid woman!" Robbie cursed. "Sometimes I find it hard to believe she and Jinty are sisters. At least Jinty had the brains and the cunning to land old Rupe. So where *did* you disappear to?"

"Boyd and I went for a stroll."

Robbie gave a low whistle, pregnant with meaning. "No wonder Tonya tore after you."

"Why is that exactly?" she asked, feigning ignorance.

"Sweetie, there's no way you can fool me. You've loved Boyd since you were a little girl. Now you're a beautiful woman. Boyd has made it pretty clear he can see that."

"And it will come to nothing," Leona said fatalistically.

"I don't agree with that at all." Robbie cut any further protests short. "You're special. Think Boyd doesn't know that? Just don't let him share your bed until you're well and truly married. I know plenty of girls who have blown their chances."

"I'll keep that in mind, Robbie," Leona said, thumping her hand on his arm.

They had reached the gallery by the time Leona stopped to take a really good look at him. He had a decided pallor. "What's wrong?" she asked worriedly. "You're deathly pale. You simply can't drink too much, Robbie."

Robbie shut his eyes. "Robbie?" She shook his arm.

"God, hell, no!" he replied. It wasn't blasphemy. It sounded more like a plea for forgiveness.

"Oh, Robbie, what's happened? You're in trouble, aren't you? I just knew it." Her green eyes darkened with anxiety. "Talk to me, please." If

Robbie couldn't pull himself together he had an uncertain future. That was the very last thing she wanted for him. "Here, come into the bedroom." She all but pulled him through her bedroom door.

"Don't leave the door open," Robbie warned, slumping into an ornate Louis chair. "Jinty's efforts at redecorating are atrocious," he moaned. "That bed, for one, is utterly ridiculous." He lowered his head into his hands.

"Forget the bed. What's wrong with you? Is there anything I can get you?"

"I'm not drunk, Leo. I know better than to break Rupe's house rules," he said, then broke into a wild laugh that had nothing to do with humour.

"Oh, Robbie, you're breaking my heart. What is it?" Leona went to him, laying her hand gently on his head. "Whatever it is, you can tell me. We'll face it together."

"I don't think even *you* will forgive me this, Leo," Robbie said, looking soulfully up at her. "I'll never forgive myself. I must be bad. And mad. Carlo, after all, was a scoundrel."

"Carlo wasn't a scoundrel." Leona surprised herself by coming to Carlo's defence. "I've always had the feeling that your father was badly maligned by Delia," she said. "She found it useful to denigrate him so she could get sympathy from the family. If I were you I'd look him up. I don't believe Carlo was anywhere near as bad as your mother makes out. She's a very devious and manipulative woman."

"And you're not exaggerating," Robbie moaned. "But I do carry some Mafia genes." He reached inside his breast pocket and, to Leona's horror and amazement, withdrew Jinty's diamond earrings.

Leona was so shocked she said absolutely nothing. Then, after a moment, she gave a little sobbing gasp, bending over and clutching her breast as though she had taken a bullet right to the heart. "Robbie…Robbie…Robbie! What were you thinking? You're going to have to explain. Have you completely lost your mind?"

"Possibly temporary insanity," Robbie groaned, feeling a tidal wave of guilt and remorse. "I live among all these filthy rich people and I can't change places with a one of them. Money corrupts, Leo. It seduces. It leads you into temptation. And finally sin."

Leona stared down at him, her blood running icy-cold. "We have to get them back," she said decisively. "You saw Jinty put them into the Limoges bowl?"

"An incredibly stupid thing to do," Robbie muttered, as though Jinty's stupidity lessened his own crime.

"Nowhere near as stupid as your lifting them," she said. "What did you think you were going to do with them? The Blanchard Diamonds are famous."

Robbie slumped even further. "I told you I went cuckoo. It's a bloody nightmare. It didn't take me a moment more to come to my senses, I swear. I was desperate to find you, only you'd disappeared."

"And what was I supposed to do, put them back?" Leona asked incredulously. "I've spoilt you rotten, Robbie. I'm your sister. I've always tried to be there for you, and you go and do a thing like that to the Blanchards—Rupert will have you hanged."

"Good thing they don't hang people any more." Robbie gave a hollow laugh. "Forgive me, Leo. It was a mad moment over which I had no control. I wanted to get back at them. Most of them treat me like I'm dirt beneath their feet."

"Oh, stop feeling sorry for yourself," Leona flashed, then she went to him and took the earrings out of his clenched hand. "I have to get these back. And I have to do it right away."

Instantly Robbie rose to his feet, his face ashen. "I can't let you do that, Leo. It's time to be a man. I'll find Boyd. I'll explain what happened. He'll tell me what a bloody fool I am—tear strips off me—but he'll work it out."

"Not Boyd," Leona said. "We can't involve Boyd in this. I'll do it. They've all retired for the night."

"What if Jinty has already gone to collect the earrings and found them missing?" Robbie spoke with quiet horror, scratching a sharp finger down his cheek and leaving a trail of blood.

"She hasn't checked," Leona said. "She can't have. If she had, the whole house would be in an uproar."

"Hammerings on the door. The oldest rellie turfed out of bed. The likes of me strip-searched." Robbie brightened just faintly. "Let me do it."

"And what if you're caught out? No, leave it to me."

No one in the long gallery of the west wing, though the faces in the paintings stared very hard at her.

No one coming up or going down the grand staircase, unless they were the ghosts of Blanchards past. No sound of voices or footsteps either. It was as though the night had swallowed everyone up.

Leona had never felt so terrified in her life. The diamonds were freezing, like chunks of ice in her hand. The big chandeliers were off but there were still a number of lamps and sconces burning. She pressed on stealthily, quiet as a mouse, if ever a mouse would have been allowed to take up residence in such a house.

What if she met up with someone—Rupert? She didn't think she could deal with that. Rupert was famous for appearing when least wanted or expected. What excuse would she have for coming downstairs again? A book from the library, perhaps? Who would possibly swallow that? Maybe an insomniac who read until sunrise? Could she say she had lost one of her own earrings? Danger in that. She was wearing them, for one thing, and the very mention of earrings would be sure to alert Rupert, who was equally famous for his sweeping powers of deduction.

God, she felt sick. Sick and shuddering with nerves. For a moment, she stood outside the drawing room, trying to sense if anyone was inside. Not that they would be in there singing songs. She glanced in quickly, then out again. How could Robbie have done such a lunatic thing? It was wrong, wrong, wrong and he would have been made to pay for it. Rupert, beneath the cultivated veneer, was a hard man. Maybe cruel. He certainly hadn't made Aunt Alexa happy.

By now she was convinced there was no one in the drawing room. A few lamps had been left on in there as well. But everything was very still. So still. Distressed, worried sick for Robbie, sick for herself, she moved into the beautiful quiet room like a girl with wings. She had taken the precaution of removing her high heeled evening sandals, replacing them with a pair of ballet-style flats. Now her footsteps on the carpet were soundless.

So far, so good!

Yet she felt like a thief, guilty as sin. Her heart was pounding so hard it had all but jumped into her throat. At any moment she expected Rupert or Jinty to materialise like a couple of sleuths hard on her tracks. She had to move faster. Finally she reached the little gilded table, putting out a trembling hand... *Please, God, help me do this.* But would or should God extricate her from sin?

"Leo?" a voice that surely wasn't God's said from behind her, making her jump. "What are you doing downstairs? Couldn't you sleep?"

Tears pulsed in her eyes. She couldn't seem to breathe as the anguish and humiliation rolled over her. The game was up.

"Leo?" Boyd said again. "Are you okay?"

He sounded very concerned. What should she say? No, I'm not okay. And I never will be again. Should she spin around, hold the diamonds out to him with a jaunty, I couldn't resist taking them. Now I'm trying to put them back. The family might destroy Robbie but Boyd would never destroy her. He most certainly would be shocked and appalled, but she knew he wouldn't turn her in. Boyd wasn't Rupert. He had a huge reservoir of heart.

At this point, perplexed and intrigued, Boyd, who had come downstairs to turn off lights, moved purposefully towards her. His strong hands descended on her delicate shoulders, bare except for plaited wisps of chiffon that served as straps. Slowly he turned her to face him, conscious that she was scarcely breathing. "Tell me what's the matter." Urgently he searched her face.

"Nothing," she whispered, averting her red-gold head.

"There must be something. What have you got in your hand?"

"Nothing."

He looked at her in disbelief. "Of course you have." He reached down to take hold of her hand and, as he did so, it went nerveless and the diamond earrings rolled out of her grasp and onto the exquisite Savonnerie rug, the diamonds all the while shooting out brilliant white lights.

"This isn't possible!" Boyd groaned, bending to retrieve them.

"I don't know what came over me." Her voice shook. She was shaking all over.

"Well, I do." Boyd began to ease her backwards into an armchair. "What the hell is going on here? Robbie's in trouble. Surely to God he didn't think stealing the earrings was a way out?"

This was horrible. He suspected Robbie already. "It had nothing to do with Robbie," she said, vehemently shaking her head.

"So you stole them, did you?" he asked, his voice full of disbelief and disgust.

"It was a moment of madness, Boyd. I wanted to try them on. I *knew* I had to return them. That's what I was trying to do. You mustn't have noticed, but Jinty took them off towards the end of the evening and put them in the Limoges bowl."

"Ah!" He considered that for a moment. "So recount your movements for me, if you would. At what late point of the evening did you make your move? Let's see, you were in the garden with me, getting kissed senseless. Then you said your goodnights and went up to bed. I saw you and Robbie going up the stairs together. Robbie, your 'kid brother'."

"I'm telling you the truth, Boyd." She looked up at him, looming so tall above her, with huge anguished eyes.

"No, Leona, you're telling me one big fat lie. Why didn't you just come to me? Then you wouldn't have had to do this. Why didn't Robbie have the guts to come to me and confess?"

"Robbie had nothing to do with it," she repeated. She stood a better chance than Robbie.

"Oh, stop it!" Boyd said, as though he'd totally run out of patience. How formidable he looked! How handsome! He had taken off his jacket but he was still in his evening clothes, the collar of his white shirt undone, his black dress tie hanging loose.

"Someone's coming!" Leona gave a terrified gasp, starting up in alarm. She looked towards the entrance hall.

Boyd didn't reply. He grabbed her as if she were

a doll, hauling her back against the green and gold curtains. "Kiss me," he ordered bluntly. "Kiss me and make it good!"

She did exactly as he told her, a captive in his powerful embrace. Their mouths locked in a kiss that, strategy or not, deepened and deepened until her brain turned to mush and she was moaning his name.

"Well, this *is* a surprise!" Jinty stalked into the room like a goddess of the hunt who had caught up with her prey.

Leona couldn't speak for the life of her. It was left to Boyd to query smoothly, "Surprise? It can't be that big a surprise, Jinty. I've always had deep feelings for Leona and she for me."

Jinty's determined jaw set in unflattering lines. "If I recall correctly, you and Chloe Compton are to make a match of it." She sounded chilly and utterly shocked.

"That might be *Dad's* plan," Boyd said, "but not mine. I make my own decisions, Jinty. I thought you knew that. I'm no more in love with Chloe than—who shall I say?—I'm in love with your sister, Tonya. Oh, by the way—" Boyd keeping one arm around the deeply trembling Leona, dug the other hand into his trouser pocket "—you really shouldn't leave extremely valuable heirloom jewellery lying around. Is that why you came downstairs?"

Jinty's skin flushed as if she were in disgrace. "You have my earrings?"

"I have the *family* earrings, Jinty," Boyd said pointedly, swiftly seizing the advantage. "They will eventually come to my wife. It's a good thing I happened to notice where you put them." He held the earrings out to her and Jinty moved forward to take them, her features sharply honed with all manner of emotions.

"I'd appreciate it if you didn't say anything to your father," she said stiffly.

"Jinty, I wouldn't dream of telling him. Just be a little more careful with them in future."

Jinty, diamonds in hand, turned to go. "I may be a little slow," she said, "but I had no idea what was going on with you and Leona."

"But nothing *has* been going on, as you put it," Boyd assured her. "Not until this weekend. I was giving Leo a little time, that's all. She's been enjoying her career. I'm sure we're all very proud of her, but now I've decided we have to get on with the rest of our lives."

"Does your father know any of this?" Jinty asked through clenched teeth. It was obvious she had difficulty speaking she was so clearly stunned.

"Not as yet. He's been too busy trying to push Chloe at me. I'll tell him when I'm ready. Leona will make the most beautiful bride."

Jinty couldn't get out of the drawing room fast enough.

* * *

"Has everyone taken leave of their senses?" Leona asked when she was quite sure that Jinty had gone up the staircase.

"Well, I'm certainly in possession of mine," Boyd said. "We'd better get you upstairs before you collapse. And you could tell that cowardly little brother of yours—"

"He's not a coward," she said loyally. "He wanted to return the earrings to the Limoges bowl."

Boyd ignored her. "You know another thing about Robbie? He's well over his ears in debt."

"Is he?" She moaned as if it was all too much for her.

"You *don't* know?"

Her green eyes were dark with dismay. "Well…he tells me everything, but…"

Boyd cut her off. "He's got himself mixed up with people who are little more than thugs. The kind who target young idiots like Robbie, a rich kid, an easy mark."

"Dear God!" Leona let her head fall into her hands. "I blame myself."

"Well, you would, wouldn't you?" Boyd returned very crisply. "You've been covering for Robbie for years. Where is he now? And don't, I beg of you, Leona, lie."

"He's in my room."

"What, hiding under the bed?"

"You know why he gets into trouble, don't

you?" Leona made a passionate effort to try to absolve Robbie from some of the blame.

"He has an identity crisis?" Boyd asked, unbearably suave.

"Yes, he does. His father deserted him. Dad doesn't know what to make of him. For heaven's sake, he doesn't know what to make of *me*. The proverbial cat would make a better mother than Delia. Robbie has suffered."

"Don't be absurd!" Boyd cut her short. "Robbie wallows in his suffering when he's being looked after very well," he told her grimly. "He has a more than adequate allowance. He buys the best of everything from Blanchards, then forgets to pay off his account. He's at university. He's a fine athlete, good-looking and clever. My heart bleeds for him."

"So what are you going to do?" she whispered.

"Oh, give me a break! I'm going to knock him senseless."

Leona winced. "You wouldn't do that." Was it possible?

"What good would that do?" Boyd shrugged. "You tell Robbie I want to meet him ten o'clock sharp tomorrow morning in the hall. We'll go for a nice long walk together."

"Oh, thank you, Boyd. Thank you." She felt like falling to her knees and kissing his hand.

"Alas, not the end of the story, Leona," he said

tersely. "I meant what I said. That wasn't a bit of play-acting for Jinty's benefit. You *will* make a beautiful bride. *My* bride. You belong to me. No one else. Consider that *our* deal. Robbie gets thrown a lifeline. But if there's a next time when he gets himself into a really bad situation, he can drown. But for now, *you* marry *me*. You're the only one who can give me what I want."

The more she scanned his dynamic face, the angrier she became. So angry she started to stutter. "So...can...you t-tell me exactly *why* you want me?" Her green eyes flashed and rosy colour swept into her face. She was maddened by his easy arrogant assumption that she would go along with his grand plan. Robbie or no Robbie, she wasn't going to accept this sort of proposal when it was clearly as he said, a *deal*.

"Is it because you think you *own* me? Or think you can. Is that it?"

For answer, he knotted his fingers through her rose-gold hair, drawing her mutinous face closer. Then he brought his masterful mouth down on hers, almost bruising in its intensity, leaving his indelible mark. "That's it," he said. "That's it exactly."

"But that's blackmail!" Her legs were buckling. The fine flavour of him was on her lips and her tongue. No matter what heart, body and spirit craved, it would be spineless to give in to him without a fight.

"You have the choice, Leona," he told her. "It's over for Robbie or we start a new life together."

It was near impossible to calm herself. "What if your father decides it simply won't do?" She knew that was bound to happen.

His expression hardened. "My private life is a no-go area where my father is concerned, Leona. *I* pick my wife, Leona. I choose *you*. I've known you since you were a child. I understand you better than anyone else. For your sake I'll make sure Robbie gets pulled very firmly into line. And it will go no further. In my view, Robbie is more pampered than suffering and it has to stop." He sounded so incredibly stern she could have wept.

"How long have you been thinking about this?" she asked, considering with a rush of horror that it might be one way of getting rid of *all* the women who were chasing him.

"Does it make a difference?" he asked suavely. "Let's just say tonight has brought things to a head. No need for you to say anything to anyone. Not just now, anyway. I'll handle all the preliminaries."

"Preliminaries? What the heck does that mean?" she asked fiercely, her redhead's temper coming to the fore. "And what if I don't go along with it all? You'll throw Robbie to the lions?"

"I should have threatened to throw him to the lions sooner," Boyd answered very crisply. "But you *will* go along with it, so we no longer have to consider it. I'll speak to my father some time this weekend."

"Not frightened of anyone, are you?" she said caustically. "Well, *I* am. Please wait until I make my getaway before you speak to Rupert. He'll be furious."

"Are you sure you've got that right?" He was staring down at her with his bluer than blue eyes.

"Of course I've got it right," she retorted, frowning at the question. "Little Leo stealing his precious son away?" She was trying very hard to stare him down, but she couldn't.

"Why are you trying so hard to throw up excuses?" A vertical line appeared between his black brows. "You're beautiful. You're clever. You can be a handful, like now. But, that aside, you're a real asset to the family. Any family. So why are you so incredibly insecure?"

She flushed with anger. "Maybe it's an age thing," she threw back with intense emotion. "You've got problems too, though God knows you've got the capacity to go about solving them. I'm twenty-four. You're thirty. One can gain a lot of experience in six years."

"You're suggesting I wait until you're thirty?"

"Thirty is fine for you."

"I want you *now*, Leo," he said. "You're off your head if you think I'm going to give you even another year. Make it six months."

That nearly knocked her out. "You sound absolutely mad."

He sighed deeply. "No one but no one can make me as mad as you."

"Yet you're talking about marrying me. Let's make it clear. Do we live together or do we retain separate apartments?"

"Well, it's an idea," he said, then began to laugh. "Don't you think I can make you happy, Flower Face?"

She looked away from him, fighting tears. "The thing is, Boyd, you can overlook the need for *love*. Okay, I know we've got an emotionally charged relationship. You say you want me. I'm frightened to admit that I want you too. But you're not the first man to tell me he wanted me. I don't want to boast, but I hear it all the time. But *want*? What does that mean? Does it mean simply assuaging a sensual appetite?"

"It certainly does," he said, his voice deep and sexy. "How can it not?"

"Don't you dare laugh," she said. "You're always laughing at me. I need someone to *love* me. Really love me." She was so overwrought she was almost shouting. "Why *don't* you, Boyd?" she cried in a fresh upsurge of anguish. "There, you can't give me an answer." She totally ignored the fact that she had scarcely given him time to open his mouth. Instead, she spun like a ballet dancer, heading for the entrance hall.

"Leona!" he called after her.

His voice begged her to stop but she wasn't having a bar of it. She was a woman for whom love was all important. Boyd's love. She wasn't a commodity to be bought on the open market-place, she thought furiously. It was hellish to love someone the way she loved Boyd.

When she arrived back at her room she found Robbie pacing the carpet like a panther caught in a cage. "Well?" He turned to her with anguished eyes, no colour whatever in his cheeks.

Leona crossed the room to fall back on the bed. Her head was whirling with chaotic thoughts. She had to close her eyes and count to ten. After she did that, she said, "You're off the hook."

Robbie raised his eyes to the heavens. "Thanks be to God," he said piously. "I think I'll go back to church. You were able to put the earrings back?"

"Almost." She sat up, feeling dizzy, looking more delicately lovely than ever, her chiffon skirt spread out on either side of her.

Robbie's expression turned to one of dread. "You were caught?"

She nodded. "It happens, Robbie," she said sombrely, at the same time wanting to put him out of his misery. "Boyd chose that very moment to come downstairs to turn off the lights. He saw me in the drawing room."

"Holy Mother!" Robbie was so overtaken by weakness he had to slump down on the opulent day bed. "You must have been terrified."

Even now she couldn't suppress her feelings of panic. "Of course I was, but I felt enormous relief that it was Boyd. What if it had been Rupert?"

Robbie gave an agitated laugh. "True, we'd have had to emigrate to Antarctica. So what happened?"

"That's for *you* to find out," she said, feeling unable to explain much further. She had to sleep on Boyd's extraordinary proposal. She was already well into convincing herself that it smacked of a convenient way out for him. When they weren't striking sparks off one another, they did get along extremely well. Naturally she would in time be expected to produce an heir or heiress, so it was really a marriage of convenience. A lot of people settled for that. Rich people more than most.

"Listen, Robbie. Boyd wants you to meet him in the hall at ten o'clock sharp," she said, forcing herself upright. "The two of you are going for a little walk. You wouldn't want him swearing at you in the house."

Robbie began madly slicking his dark hair back. "Boyd doesn't swear even when he's angry. The most I've heard is the odd bloody. So you told him? Why not? I *am* to blame. I should never have let you."

"You'll be pleased to hear I didn't tell him,

Robbie," Leona said. "But Boyd knows me too well. He knows I wouldn't have taken the earrings. He guessed you had. He knows all about the bad people you're involved with."

Robbie remained very still. "So what's he going to do?" He looked straight at her, awaiting her response much as a man in the dock would await a jury's verdict.

"I've told you, Robbie. Boyd sees you as being cushioned by wealth. Now that I've been forced to think about it, you *are*. Look at that suit. It must have cost a couple of thousand. Dad gives you a comfortable allowance. You'll get your degree and, if you want it, you'll be given a good position within Blanchards. I'm very sympathetic towards your personal problems. Why wouldn't I be? I have them as well. It's the old story of an unstable childhood, but we've survived and we have so much else, after all. You have to liberate yourself, Robbie. Not keep drinking from the poisoned well. Find your father. Confront him. You could go in the summer vacation. For all you know, Carlo might be thrilled out of his mind to see you."

Robbie gave a bitter laugh. "I'll ask him why he never invited me. But the big question is—am I going to be *free* to travel? It was a very bad thing I did, taking the earrings."

"The only thing worse would've been for you to try to *wear* them," Leona said, trying for some light relief. "It *was* a bad thing, Robbie. An insane thing for someone so bright. But you didn't go through with it. That's in your favour. It was a moment of madness." Always protective towards him, Leona slid off the bed to give him a reassuring hug. "We both know Boyd is going to read you the riot act tomorrow."

"That's what I need." Robbie's voice was filled with self-disgust.

"Well, you're going to get it and it won't be pleasant. Take it on the chin. Boyd has assured me the matter will go no further."

"He'd do anything for you," Robbie said, then looked her in the eyes. "It's all about you. Did you ask him?"

Leona hesitated for only a few seconds. "Actually, he asked me to marry him." She didn't say that he had more like *informed* her they were to be married. Not the same thing at all.

Robbie's woebegone face lit up as his fears virtually disappeared. He put his hands around Leona's narrow waist and began to swing her around like a child. "But that's marvellous. Bloody marvellous! I couldn't think of anyone in the world who would be more perfect for you!"

"No thoughts there might be plenty of girls more perfect for him?" Leona asked breathlessly when he set her down again.

"No way!" Robbie exclaimed, breaking into

another delighted laugh. "You two are made for each other. Actually, I was starting to think that Boyd was taking his time."

"Wh-a-t!" Leona stared back at him, flooded with astonishment.

"Gosh, Leo, you *radiate* off one another. I'm not the only person to see it, you know."

"So who's the *other*?" she asked in amazement.

"Lots probably." Robbie shrugged. "But good old Geraldine, for one. She's a sharp old bird."

"No sharper than her brother, Rupert," Leona said. "I'd hate to see his face when he hears."

"But Rupe is very fond of you." Robbie frowned.

"Maybe he is in a way. But *not* as a match for his son."

"Sweetheart," Robbie spoke very tenderly, trying to buck her up, "if Boyd wants you, he'll have you. No one will stand in his way. Boyd's well on the way to becoming more powerful than his dear old dad. And a damn sight nicer person."

"And that wouldn't be hard."

CHAPTER FIVE

WHEN ROBBIE ARRIVED back at the house around midday he looked numb.

"Are you all right?" Concerned, Leona took him by the hand, much as she had done since he was a little boy. For a brief moment he took comfort from her presence, then he drew a deep breath, steadying himself.

"I'm fine."

"Then I'd hate to see you when you aren't." Quickly, she led him by the quietest route through the house into the garden, bypassing the terrace with its outdoor sofas, armchairs and tables where some of the family had congregated, enjoying the sunshine. A buffet lunch would be served from noon until the main event of the day, the fastest field sport in the world.

Robbie, an excellent horseman, was on Boyd's team, as was Peter and Peter's first cousin, James, through his mother's side of the family. The opposing team was made up of fine New South Wales players. But Leona was far from sure that Robbie should now play. Many polo players, like Boyd, found the element of danger alluring—as did Robbie, for that matter, but he looked as though all the stuffing had been knocked out of him. Predictably, the over-protective Leona felt upset for him, perversely blaming Boyd for having come on too strong. There was no logic to it, but Robbie brought out her protective instincts. Boyd, on the other hand, could look after himself.

When they were a distance from the house she drew him down a long pergola that had been mounted on splendid Doric stone pillars. Long tresses of the wisteria floribunda "Alba" cascaded from on high, softening the grandeur of the pillars. There was a little white trelliswork pavilion at the end of the walk, Mughal in style and embellished with a beautiful old-fashioned deep pink rose that clung to the abundant light green foliage. Here they could talk in privacy.

Robbie sat down beside her, then put his dark head into faintly trembling hands. "Thank God that's over!" Gratefully he breathed in the calming scent of the roses.

Long entrenched in the business of looking after him, Leona burst out, "Boyd must have been very tough on you."

"No more than I deserved!" Robbie sat bolt

upright, half turning to face her. "Hey, don't go blaming Boyd for anything," he exclaimed, obviously surprised and concerned that she had.

"How can I not?" she said, distressed by his appearance. "It's obvious he's knocked you for six. How can you play this afternoon? Polo is a dangerous, demanding game. You have to have all your wits about you."

"Listen, Leo, I'm playing," Robbie answered emphatically. "I wouldn't miss it for the world. I just have to regain my balance. A good lunch will help. Actually, I feel better than I have in ages. Can't you understand that? It's like going to confession and receiving absolution. Boyd was much too generous. I don't deserve it. He'll get the bad guys off my back. He said a lot has been invested in me to succeed. He also said I have your love and loyalty—hell, he reduced me to tears about that. Anyway, I swear to you, Leo, I'm going to mend my ways. I'm going to turn over a new leaf. I'm going to make you and Boyd proud of me. I know I've caused you a lot of anxiety and I've leant on you terribly. That has to stop. *Both* of us have to stop seeing me as your 'kid brother'."

"Boyd said that, did he?" She bit her lip.

"It's true, isn't it?" Robbie appealed to her. "Why are you trying to find fault with Boyd in this? He's my saviour. I thought you loved him. You told me you were getting married." He took hold of her arm. "Hell, *I* didn't have anything to do with this sudden decision, did I?"

"Of course you didn't." Leona stopped that idea in its tracks. "It's just that I see Boyd as invincible."

"We all die, Leo," Robbie said gently.

She shivered in the golden heat. "Don't talk about dying!" For Boyd to die would destroy her. "It's just I've spent so many years—"

"Putting up a front with Boyd?" Robbie suggested. "In some ways I think you find loving him the way you do terrifying," he added very perceptively.

"Isn't love terrifying?" she asked. "Love also sets one up for loss. The bliss of my childhood was shattered by the loss of my mother. Dad turned into another person. I think he forced himself to remarry. You know, the couples thing."

"He could have done better than Mother," said Delia's only child, betraying the full extent of his emotional dislocation.

"Did Boyd say anything to you about—" she stumbled over the word "—*us?*"

"He said you'd agreed he'd make the announcement after he'd spoken to his father."

"Who won't be at all happy," Leona repeated, showing her anxiety. The last thing she wanted to do was cause big trouble. For one thing, it might rebound on her own father, who held a high position in the firm. Rupert was not a man to be crossed.

Sharp-eyed Robbie inspected his stepsister's lovely distressed face. "Why, Leo, sweetie, Boyd won't give a damn about that. I keep telling you. He loves you. You're the only woman in the world for him. Hell, I just hope I can find a woman I can love like Boyd loves you. Don't you know how lucky you are?"

"Did he *say* he loved me?" Leona asked, so very uncertain of Boyd's true motives.

"Leo, he doesn't have to," Robbie said. "When have *you* ever put into words your true feelings for Boyd? You've spent your time throwing dust in his eyes. I'd say Boyd has acted admirably. He's given you an opportunity to grow up, stand on your own two feet, carve out a career. He's very proud of you. We all are. Who cares about old Rupe? To be honest, I don't think Boyd cares a lot about him either. Well, he *is* his father, but I have the feeling Boyd has never forgiven Rupe for the hard time he gave his mother. I do remember Aunt Alexa as being the loveliest lady and so kind to me. Then old Rupe ups and marries that gold-digger, Jinty. How he could after losing a woman like Alexa, I'll never know."

Leona didn't know either. "For someone who is only twenty, you're very perceptive, Robbie," she said.

"That's true." He took the compliment for a statement of fact. "How did beautiful Alexa marry that wicked man? It couldn't have been the money. Alexa's family is old money, establishment."

"In case you haven't noticed, Rupert is still a handsome, virile man," Leona said wryly. "If Jinty left him tomorrow—"

"That will *never* happen," Robbie assured her."Being Mrs Rupert Blanchard counts for everything in Jinty's world. I bet she's cursing the day Oz cut away from the Queen's Honours system. She could have been Lady Blanchard. Now, wouldn't that be something?"

"Actually, there is a Lady Blanchard," Leona said, referring to the English side of the family. "But my point is that Rupert could have his pick of goodness knows how many women. Some as young as me."

"Then it's really a form of prostitution, isn't it?" Robbie opined. "Selling yourself for money."

Leona swallowed. "Well, I suppose that's one way to put it."

"It could never be you." Robbie turned to her with his flashing white smile. "You and Boyd are not like them. You're marrying for love. Hell, I feel like dancing!" He jumped up and held out his hand. "Come on. Let's go back to the house. I'm starving."

The three polo fields received constant year round attention from Rupert's groundsmen to keep the surfaces in fine playing condition. With the more than welcome spring rains, Polo One, with perhaps the most spectacular setting, surrounded by rolling hills and magnificent shady trees was looking in great shape. A crowd of spectators from near and far was seated on rugs, collapsible chairs, bonnets, boots of cars, cushions and so on, right around the field. Those who weren't early enough to find the choicest spots beneath the trees made sure they brought big beach umbrellas to ward off the brilliant sun.

Each team was made up of four players, wearing a different coloured jersey, bearing the number of the position they were playing. Robbie, who had made a lightning recovery, was wearing a green Number 1 jersey, which meant he was the most offensive player. Peter Blanchard was Number 4, primarily responsible for defending his team's goal. Peter's cousin, James, was at Number 2. James was more experienced than either Robbie or Peter. Boyd, as team captain, wore a deep red jersey that for some reason made his eyes look bluer than ever. Boyd, with an impressive armoury of strokes, was the highest rated player so he had the pivotal position of Number 3.

Leona, pre-match, moved freely about the gathering, greeting and being greeted by the familiar polo crowd. All four men on the Blanchard team looked stunningly handsome in their gear, a thought she was not alone in having; the tight-fitting white trousers, coloured jerseys, high boots, knee guards and helmets gave them the glamour of men in uniform. The opposing team looked pretty dashing too. To make it even better for the young female spectators, six of the eight players were bachelors.

In a cordoned off area beneath the deep shade of the trees were the polo ponies. A great polo pony was essential to a fine player's performance and proficiency. The Blanchard team was superbly mounted. There were twenty-four ponies in all, mostly mares, that had to be made available during a match, due to the extreme demands put on a pony during the six period chukkas. Four minute breaks were taken to enable the players to change ponies.

Polo, one of the fastest, roughest, most dangerous games in the world of sport, was thus a rich man's game. The upkeep of the teams of ponies alone was sufficient to keep it that way.

Leona was nervous. Nervous and excited too. She loved the game—the speed and athleticism of horse and rider, the strategies the brilliant pivotal players, like Boyd, came up with to clinch a game. But she had two men in her life to worry about. Boyd and Robbie. Dangerous collisions could and did happen even with the "right of way" rule. Robbie, though a fine player, was known on occasion to be downright reckless. Boyd, an even better rider, the far more experienced, subtle and considered player, was nonetheless given to spectacular displays especially on his number one polo pony, the beautiful mare, Andromeda, in play today. Robbie's opposite number was a player Leona had watched many times before. Without question an experienced player with a big range of shots, he wasn't above a bit of barging, hooking and blocking his opposite number to slow him down. Mostly it worked. So there was a duel on there. Even Boyd, who relied on thought, action and fantastic speed as opposed to dirty tactics, which actually made him the superior opponent, when the chips were down played his team to win.

Leona was wearing white—always good in the heat—a pinstriped fine cotton shirt with matching crisp white trousers, an eye-catching navy and white leather belt looped through the waistband. To complete the look she had brushed her hair high off her forehead, then caught it into an updated French pleat. She looked, as she always did, very chic. It was, after all, part of her job and so far as the family was concerned that was the way they wanted and expected to see her. Rupert had already complimented her on her appearance and kissed her on both cheeks. Obviously his son and heir hadn't got around to having that heart-to-heart talk. Well, she *had* told Boyd she wanted to be well clear of Brooklands when that happened.

Jinty had had the good sense to keep a still tongue in her head, not wanting to fall out with the Heir.

Tonya, though, as always, had a jibe to share. "Don't you find white a problem?" she smirked, inspecting Leona from head to toe, immensely jealous and agitated by the way Leona's slender figure and glowing head was soaking up all the sunlight.

"I'm not going to dig the garden beds, Tonya," was Leona's reply, her tone pleasant. Keeping one's cool in the face of Tonya's contrived insults and barbs only served to irritate Tonya the more. Tonya herself was looking bone thin but very stylish in a deceptively simple shift dress, its colour almost a match with Boyd's red jersey.

Robbie, then Peter, came up to Leona, expecting and getting good luck and best wishes for a win. Peter put his arm tightly around her in some sort of claim, before his kiss landed on the side of her mouth, despite her best attempt to dodge it.

Nevertheless she knew the clinch would set off a chain of gossip. She remembered how one elderly member of the family had had a girl pregnant from a single kiss she'd caught one of the cousins exchanging with his then girlfriend. "Such things do happen!" was the dire warning.

"That boy's in love with you," Geraldine now told her, shaking her arm as if to put her on the alert.

"What a lot of rot, Gerri!" Leona tried to answer carelessly.

"Not rot, my dear," Geraldine corrected her firmly. "Just be sure to tell him you're spoken for."

Spoken for? Leona felt the hot wave of colour stain her cheeks. "Are you going to tell me how you heard that?" Boyd was very close to his aunt. He must have told her.

"I've heard nothing. So far," Geraldine maintained, adjusting the brim of her straw hat to a snappier angle. "I have *eyes*."

Leona fell into the deckchair beside her, urgently taking Geraldine's hand. "So what exactly is it you think you've seen? And with whom?"

Geraldine patted the small fine-boned hand that held hers. Then her shrewd grey eyes went past Leona's lovely, imploring face. "He's coming over right now. Don't look so worried, child. I've had my suspicions for quite a while."

"Oh, my goodness!" Leona jumped up, stopping only to whisper in Geraldine's ear, "Gerri, I swear I'm frightened of you."

"Don't be frightened, child," Geraldine looked up with a reassuring smile. "Everything will be fine."

All it would need was a miracle.

"Flower Face, still running away?" Boyd swiftly caught up with her as she dodged through the trees, catching hold of her hand.

"I have to, Boyd. I'm feeling absolutely stretched." Indeed she was. She rounded to stare up into his sapphire eyes, gem-like against his bronzed skin.

"You want us to have a nice quiet game?" he asked with such a beguiling half smile.

"Damn it! The game's only half of it," she said

spiritedly. "I am nervous for you and Robbie. I couldn't bear it if either of you were injured."

"For heaven's sake, I thought all your thoughts were with Peter!" he scoffed. "Where does he get off, hugging you like that? I was gratified to see you turn your head away. He was most certainly aiming for an off-to-the-wars type kiss."

"Well, he didn't get it!" Leona said in a tart voice. "Have you said anything at all to Gerri about... about...us?"

"One would have to get up very early in the morning to take Gerri by surprise," Boyd said. "Gerri's a mind-reader. Why, has she said something?"

Leona bit her lip. "She said everything will be fine."

"And so it will," he said. "So, are you going to wish me luck?" Those blue eyes sparkled a challenge at her.

"Think you're clever, don't you?" she muttered. On impulse, she reached up and pulled his shining blue-black head down to her. "Good luck, *darling* Boyd," she crooned in a sweet seductive voice, her green eyes alight with malice. With infinite gentleness she cupped his dynamic face in her hands, then she kissed him squarely on his sardonic mouth.

There! Served him right! She never could resist his dares.

* * *

On her way back to her chair, Leona ignored the expressions on the faces all around her. Some were soft with astonishment, others hard with calculation. The family was already divided in its opinion of Leona and Boyd as a couple.

"Think you're a siren, don't you?" Tonya, frowning fiercely in the grip of jealousy, hissed at her as Leona passed close by. "Don't get your hopes up. You'll never lure Boyd."

"Still, he's just *wonderful* to kiss," Leona pretended to gush, hastening to take her place beside Gerri. The match was due to start.

Robbie, nicely set up by his captain, scored the first two goals.

"Oh, jolly well played!" Geraldine clapped enthusiastically. "Of course it was Boyd, the tactician, who turned the play to offence, but I must say Roberto responded brilliantly. I'm just loving this. Rupert was a darn fine player. But you wouldn't remember all that well, would you, dear?"

"Of course I do," Leona said. Rupert, approaching sixty, had been warned off the game by his doctor after a number of bone shattering "bumps" and one crashing fall in his late forties.

"Didn't have Boyd's finesse, though," Geraldine further commented.

As the match progressed it became apparent that it was a duel of wits between Boyd, captain of the

Red Team, and Bart Ellory, captain of the Blue Team, the two most experienced players on the field. From time to time Leona found herself with a clenched fist to her mouth, while Geraldine persisted in jumping to her feet at her nephew's heroic deeds. The crowd was getting a superlative display of horsemanship and polo sense. Given yet another opportunity for scoring by his captain, Robbie got set for a full free swing, his team mate Peter wisely giving him plenty of room. A few seconds more and Robbie put the ball across the goal line, bringing the crowd to its feet. At half-time the score was six-three for the home team. The second half promised to be a cliff-hanger.

"I don't know that my heart can take it!" Leona said, accepting the cold glass of sparkling lime and lemon that was handed to her. What a day! Just how many people had seen her kiss Boyd? How many more had heard about it since? Rupert was sitting with his cronies some small distance away. Eventually, Leona supposed, it would get to him.

What form would his outrage take? Leona was forced to ask herself the question.

Just minutes before full-time, facing a two-pronged attack, a member of the Blue Team frustrated by Boyd's superior speedier game, suddenly created a hazardous situation when he crossed the line setting up an inevitable collision and a certain foul that would result in a penalty. Leona didn't want to look but she couldn't turn away either. Her heart had jumped into her mouth and a wave of sickness welled up from the pit of her stomach. Even Geraldine gasped in fright and began to wipe away the perspiration that broke out on her face with a lace trimmed handkerchief.

Boyd's control of himself and his mount was nothing short of superhuman. Somehow, he managed to pull out of what looked like an imminent spill.

"You can breathe again, lovey," Geraldine instructed Leona, still gasping from the near miss.

Is anyone I love safe? Leona asked herself. Only that day she had called Boyd invincible. Well, she had been made to suffer for it. Boyd was the heart of her. The meaning of everything.

The silent crowd broke out into such applause that it bounced off the hills as the whistle blew, announcing a win for the Red Team. Now for the lavish afternoon tea with all the trimmings. It was Leona's experience that most people ate everything on offer. Her own stomach was so upset she didn't think she could touch even a cupcake. A cup of coffee, however, would go down well.

By sundown just about everyone had headed off home, the outside spectators as well as family.

"What about lunch soon?" Robbie asked as they walked to his car.

"What, egg and lettuce sandwiches on a park bench?" she joked.

"The Harbour Master?" Robbie suggested.

"Fine!" She nodded abstractedly.

"So you've decided to tough it out?" Robbie studied her face. She looked very pale but resolute.

"Well, I've never thought of myself as a coward, Robbie. If Boyd is going to tell his father, I feel I should be here. If he doesn't want me by his side, at least I can be outside the study door."

"Leo, sweetie, this isn't a tragedy!" Robbie tried to comfort her. He had never seen Leo like this before and it bothered him. "I mean, you haven't been knocked up or anything. Have you?"

She shook her head in utter disbelief. "I'll pretend you never said that, Robbie."

"Sorry, sorry," he apologised. "I know that was totally out of line. I'm only trying to say…"

She cut him off mid-sentence. "I know what you're trying to say."

"Then don't look so sad. Boyd chose *you*. That says it all, don't you think? Rupe, wicked old tyrant that he is, won't be able to sway him. You *know* Boyd. He's his own man. Why, any other girl would be over the moon."

"Why wouldn't they be?" Leona smiled wanly. So why did she feel as if she had stepped into a minefield?

* * *

Boyd was actively searching for her by the time she made her way back into the house.

"Where have you been?" He moved swiftly towards her, blue eyes searing her to the spot so she couldn't run off. "You wouldn't have gone without saying goodbye to me, would you?" he asked.

"I'm not going anywhere," she said, straightening her delicate shoulders to confront him. "If you're going to speak to your father, I feel I should be here."

His expression lightened, like the sun coming out from behind clouds. "Leo, my love, you're made of the right stuff." He bent his dark head to kiss her cheek. Just a kiss on the cheek induced delicious shudders. "But you don't have to do this. Not yet. This is my father's house. I have to remember that. We both know he's always refused to countenance any change to his plans."

"I'm the very last daughter-in-law Rupert will want or expect." Even Boyd couldn't deny it.

Boyd, perhaps fearing they might be overheard, suddenly bundled her into the drawing room. "We've been through this before, Leo, and I don't want to go through it again. It's *you* I want. End of story. We had a deal, remember?"

"An indecent deal, some might say," she said, puffing a few tendrils of hair off her heated forehead.

Boyd muffled an exasperated oath beneath his breath. "So you want to back out?"

"Then I suppose you'll have Robbie detained before he's halfway home?" she flared.

"A deal is a deal," Boyd reminded her, looking every inch the acting CEO of Blanchards. "I don't want a life without you. If you're honest with yourself, *you* don't want a life without *me*."

He was exactly right but, before Leona could say so, they were interrupted. They both spun as Jinty, her sister at her shoulder, sailed into the room. "Tonya is off," she said, as though Tonya was their very favourite person.

But Tonya was staring at them both as though they were aliens. "What's going on here?"

"Honestly, Tonya, have you never considered a career in the police force?" Boyd asked.

Tonya's sharp-featured face clouded over as she studied the striking tableau before her.

"Tonya!" Jinty, who was teetering between anger and embarrassment, cast her socially inept sister a warning glance.

Tonya either missed it or elected to take no notice. "Isn't this just too thrilling! It *is* true, isn't it?"

"I'm afraid so," Boyd said in mock sympathy.

Tonya stepped around her more substantial sister, who was trying to block her way. "She's pregnant, is she? I mean, that would be the only way."

Jinty snorted loudly, wondering what further damage her sister could inflict, but Boyd's handsome face darkened and his voice, though he didn't raise it, sounded like a call to war. "Jinty, would you please take your appalling sister out of this house? She could be in some danger."

Jinty didn't hesitate. She grabbed Tonya's arm, applying considerable pressure. "Out we go, Tonya. Out, out, I say! But, before we go, I expect you to apologise for that unforgivable remark."

"The hell I will!" a distraught, bitterly angry Tonya ranted. "All this time Rupert's sweet little Leo with her red-gold curls and her big green eyes has had her eye on the pot of gold."

"Pot of gold! Is that what I am?" Boyd asked and gave an ironic laugh. "Try to get control of yourself, Tonya. Make the effort."

"I said come with me, Tonya." Jinty's voice rose, near to a screech. "I've been praying for years and years you'd learn how to keep your stupid mouth shut, but it has all been for nothing."

"But you've said yourself—" Tonya started to protest, but Jinty gave her a furious push ahead.

"Unbelievable!" Boyd muttered as they moved out of the door, Tonya dissolving into wails.

And that wasn't the end of it.

Rupert suddenly appeared, looking deeply irritated—something he did very well. "What on earth's going on?" he asked, staring towards the front door. "Was that my wife I heard screeching? Or was it one of the peacocks?" Peacocks did, in fact, roam the estate.

"It was Jinty," Boyd confirmed. "Tonya put her in a very bad mood." When his father didn't respond, Boyd asked, "It was you who dumped Tonya on us?"

"You can't dictate to me, Boyd. This is my house, might I remind you?" Rupert returned with supreme arrogance.

"The house *is* yours as the current custodian," Boyd flashed back. "The house then passes to me. I've told you before, Tonya is a born trouble-maker. One wonders why you choose to ignore it."

"Oh, she's harmless." Rupert threw up his hands. "Besides, Jinty likes her here," he said with dizzying untruth.

"Jinty is as unhappy to see Tonya as the rest of us," Boyd flatly contradicted. "If you have the time, Leona and I would like to speak to you."

"Certainly, certainly." Rupert was now at his most affable. "Come back to the study. What's it about? Leo has already had a big promotion. One step at a time now, Leo." He wagged a finger at her. "You're only twenty-three, aren't you?"

"Twenty-four, Rupert," Leona said, marvelling that her voice sounded so composed.

"You're not going to tell me you're thinking of getting engaged?" He swung round to beam at her. "Young Peter, is it?" he asked conspiratorially.

"Young Boyd," Boyd corrected very dryly, making the position manifestly clear.

Rupert stopped dead, just outside the open study door. "Is this some sort of joke?" His black brows rose and before Leona's very eyes he turned into Geraldine's tyrannosaurus.

"Why don't we go inside?" Boyd suggested, clearly unimpressed by his father's shape shifting. But the strain was showing on Leona. She was trembling. Rupert broke people. He was ruthless when crossed. Everyone in and outside the business world knew that. What about her father's job? Rupert could sack her father on some pretext. Being a billionaire with vast holdings both at home and abroad would give any human being way too much power.

In brooding silence Rupert took a seat behind his massive partner's desk. He kept his handsome head down. He didn't look up. His blood pressure must have shot up because his face was very flushed.

Boyd saw Leona seated in a leather armchair, then he took the one beside her. "I can't believe it's such a shock to you, Dad. You don't miss much. I know you and the Comptons have foolishly set your hearts on an alliance between our families, the thinking being that one family fortune is great, two is even better. Just like the Middle Ages. Chloe is a nice girl. I'm fond of her. She'll make someone an excellent wife, but that someone surely isn't *me*."

That statement appeared to anger Rupert beyond words. He stuck out his bottom lip with the utmost belligerence. "What are you telling me?" He stared balefully at his son.

"It would be better for all if you could learn to accept that I make my own decisions, Dad," Boyd said quietly. "Leona is the woman for me."

Rupert stared back almost wildly. "She's not a woman. She's a girl. She's your cousin. She's family. I tell you, I simply won't have it."

"Rupert, please!" Leona's voice begged for calm.

"You stay out of this, Leo," Rupert thundered, shooting an intimidating glance at her.

"I was only going to say you shouldn't allow yourself to get so angry," Leona spoke up bravely. "You've gone very red in the face."

"It's a wonder I'm not purple!" Rupert bellowed. "I thought you were different, but you're like every other goddammed female."

"That's enough, Dad," Boyd said, rising to his feet. "I consider myself honoured that Leona has consented to marry me. And, I have to tell you, she needed persuading."

Rupert swore violently.

"Okay, that's it! We're done here!" Boyd put out a hand to Leona. "Come on, sweetheart, we're going."

She took Boyd's hand. "What have you got against me, Rupert?" she asked as Boyd started to draw her away. "Is there something I should know about? You may be disappointed that Boyd won' fall in with your plans, but you're much *more* than disappointed, aren't you? You find the idea *intolerable*. What is the real reason you're so angry? There has to be one."

"Don't do it," Rupert said, looking fiercely into her eyes. "And that's an order." His voice was harsh with authority. "If you know what's good for you, your father and that upstart Robbie, you'll do as I say." As he spoke the blood was draining from his face, leaving a marked pallor. He looked far from a well man. Indeed, he looked as if he was suffering a psychotic episode.

"What the hell's going on here?" Boyd demanded, brilliant blue eyes narrowing to slits.

For answer, Rupert lifted his heavy head, laughing darkly. "You'll be waiting a long time before you'll take the reins from me, my son!"

Arrogance, but the arrogance of achievement, settled on Boyd like a cloak. "I've as good as taken over the reins now, might I remind you, Dad? How could you threaten Leo and her family in such a way? I can tell you now you'll have me to deal with if you try to hurt them in any way. You may be put out by our decision—you've spent a lifetime imposing your will on us all—but this time you won't get anyone to back you. The family is very happy with me in the driver's seat. So are the shareholders. So were you, for that matter. Leona is, by anyone's standards, a beautiful, gifted, cultivated young woman. You've always treated her most kindly. What's the huge problem now?"

"It's not a good thing for you two to marry," Rupert said rigidly, adopting his familiar autocratic tone.

Boyd tightened his hold on Leona's trembling hand. "Stop talking rubbish. You know what you're saying is ridiculous. There's no impediment whatever—legally, morally or socially—to Leona and me marrying. We're not even full second cousins. You'll have to do better than that."

Leona, mind racing, broke in, her green eyes fixed on Rupert's face. "If you think there is some impediment, Rupert, you should speak out." She could hear the fear in her own voice. Rupert's violent reaction could be carrying them into dangerous waters.

There was a long silence, during which Rupert's eyes drifted to the picture of Serena, which had hung on his wall since her death.

Leona heard the mounting anger and the challenge in Boyd's voice. "So what are you going to come up with now, Dad?" he asked with icy contempt. "Guess what, Leo's your half-sister? I wouldn't put anything past you. You'd defame Leo's dead mother. You'd defame my own beautiful mother, who had to tolerate so much from you. Only it won't wash. There *was* no affair between you and Serena, if that's what you're trying to suggest. God, you disgust me!"

Abruptly, life for Leona had moved beyond challenging. Her breath was locked in her chest. "This isn't happening, is it?" She looked to Boyd for confirmation. It came to her that he appeared much the more formidable of the two men.

"Sit down again, Leo," Boyd said, putting gentle pressure on her shoulder and easing her into her chair. "Don't let this upset you. This is only Dad playing his rotten games. He *wanted* Serena. My mother knew that. She told me years later that Dad had developed a real yen for Serena—the unobtainable—but Serena was an innocent. She didn't even know about your secret infatuation, did she, Dad? She was a young wife and mother and she and my mother were very close. Serena would never have betrayed her husband, her child or her close friend even if she had known of your aberrant feelings."

Leona's voice was little above a whisper. "No, she wouldn't have," she said. She might have been only eight, but she remembered her mother vividly—her vital presence, her wonderful sense of fun, her endless grace, her capacity for loving, their secure family unit. These attributes had informed her life. "Is that why you've been so kind to me all these years, Rupert? Because I remind you of my mother?"

"The one woman he couldn't have," Boyd said, with no sympathy at all for his father. In fact, he was staring at him with open disgust on his face. "It follows, as it does with men like Dad who spend their lives in competition with their sons, I couldn't be allowed to have you. My father is paranoid about losing. He lost my mother's love very early on. Didn't you, Dad? It took a while but then she began to see through you."

"Shut up, Boyd!" Rupert gritted, his handsome features cold and set.

"Is *that* it, Rupert?" Leona appealed to Boyd's father, sounding desolate. "You wanted to deny your own son?"

Difficult as it was to comprehend, there was a great ambivalence in Rupert Blanchard's complex nature. Existing simultaneously with a great love and pride in his son and heir was a tremendous level of competition and rivalry. That conflict had found its most powerful expression right here and now. Boyd had to be denied Leona as he had been denied Serena. Not that Serena had been aware of his illicit feelings or the conflicts within him. Rupert couldn't attempt to explain it. It just *was*.

Rupert had passed to a stage where he no longer tried to formulate answers. All his life he'd been under tremendous stress. People imagined that being a scion of the very rich was fortunate indeed. He'd had no real choices in life. His father had made it very clear to him that he was to take over Blanchards, run it with the same hard-headed skills and determination as the men of his family did. His sisters were permitted to do as they liked. Gerri had followed an academic career, while Josephine, who kept well clear of the limelight, had married her medical scientist, had four children and led a happy, fulfilled life. Not him. His beautiful Alexa had escaped him. In spirit at least. Serena had been a mid-life aberration. It could never have come to anything. But he had not forgotten. He had given Serena's daughter, Leona, her mirror image, every advantage. She was a lovely young woman in her own right. Now he was finding it unbearable for his son and Leona to be looking at him in the way that they were.

Rupert groaned aloud, then buried his face in his hands. He had always thought that he knew Alexa well, yet he had never known that she had discovered his secret infatuation. Not only that, Alexa had confided his secret to their son. Why not? Mother and son had always been very close.

The humiliation was not to be borne. Neither was it to be permitted. Rupert Blanchard reached out for a small trophy that sat on his desk, then crushed it in his bare hand.

CHAPTER SIX

As THEY CAME out of the study and walked quickly towards the entrance hall, they saw Jinty poised in an attitude of listening at the bottom of the staircase. Obviously she was wondering what was going on, so she had taken the opportunity to eavesdrop. What they didn't know was that Jinty was also taking a near primitive satisfaction in the fact that Tonya, her own sister, had missed out. Not that she had ever had a chance, but then Tonya had never really caught on to the hard realities of life.

"Is everything all right?" she asked, adopting an expression of concern. Impossible not to notice the look of strain on their faces.

"Not exactly," Boyd said, his tone almost breezy. "Dad isn't best pleased by our news."

"Did you think he would be?" Jinty asked, throwing out her hands, palms up. "He was sure you'd go for Chloe."

"Maybe not. But did he—or anyone else for that matter—*really* think I was going to go along with his plans?" Boyd gave a slight grimace. "If he's so very fond of Chloe he should divorce you, then ask Chloe to marry him. There's every chance she'll say yes."

Jinty wondered if he weren't spot on. "Actually, I rather liked Chloe," she said. "A thoroughly nice, malleable young woman, but clearly she's no match for Leo, who has so many things going for her." The merest flicker of malice. "Should I go to him?" Jinty looked from one to the other. "Be supportive?"

"Of what, Jinty?" Boyd asked, very direct. "You're going to back us, then?"

"Why, certainly!" Jinty said without a blink. "Somehow I'll make your father understand that Leo is *your* choice. Heavens, the whole time we've been married, Rupert has doted on Leo. Occasionally it has made me quite jealous. God knows it's no secret that Rupert doesn't love *me*. We rub along well together, that's all. I do have the certainty I'll be a rich woman for life but there's little in it for me of the heart. Shall I go to him?"

"Only if you want your head bitten off," Boyd replied. "Dad could do that quite easily. Incidentally, has he seen Drew Morse lately? I think he should have a check-up; his colour didn't look too good. The thing is there's no crossing Dad. He can't deal with it."

"Well, that's nothing new to me," Jinty said and briefly shut her eyes. "Rupert expects everyone to obey his every whim. Anyway, I must apologise for Tonya."

"Oh, gosh, whatever for?" Boyd asked sardonically.

"Poor Tonya never mastered the social niceties, which is one reason why she's still unmarried."

"Perhaps she should enrol in a personal development course," Boyd suggested.

Jinty blinked, then reassumed her practised smile. "Be that as it may, I do sincerely wish you and Leo the very best, Boyd. Rupert can't dictate everyone's life."

"Certainly not mine," Boyd clipped off. "Now I'm driving Leo back to Sydney. No way do I want her driving herself after an upset like that. Ask Eddie to drive her car to her apartment some time tomorrow. I'll organise someone to drive him back." He glanced down at the silent Leo, who was looking and feeling shell-shocked. "We'll collect our luggage and be off. Where shall we leave Leo's keys, Jinty?"

"On the console table, please," Jinty said, gesturing. She was already starting to walk down the corridor that led to her husband's inner sanctum. "I have my own fears for Rupert's health," she paused to confide. "He drinks far more than is good for him and I can't get him off his infernal cigars."

"Picked up the habit from his own father and his father before him," Boyd said, still scanning Leona's pale face. "Let's collect the luggage." He spoke to her quietly. "I can't wait to get out of this place."

"Where are we going?" They were driving into Sydney before Leona came out of her reverie—a long internal dialogue that had never stopped.

Boyd was staring straight ahead. He too had been very quiet on the trip, which seemed to have taken record time.

"My place," he said briefly.

For once Leona didn't argue.

Fifteen minutes later they slid into the underground car park of Boyd's grand old apartment building, which had undergone mammoth restoration only a few years before. Boyd had the penthouse, which was actually two units that had been turned into a very spacious unified whole. She had never been to the penthouse on her own but she had been invited many times to his dinner parties.

In silence they took the lift to the top, Leona not even knowing what she was doing. She felt so dazed and astounded by both Boyd's and Rupert's disclosures that she had difficulty taking it all in. It seemed to her like something out of a blockbuster novel filled with family secrets, money, sex and complex people with passionate unfulfilled yearnings. Or did novels only mirror real life? She had always known that Alexa's marriage had been unhappy, but never in a million years would she have suspected that Rupert had fallen blindly in love, however briefly, with her own mother, Serena. Yet Boyd had known and he had never said a word.

Until tonight.

No wonder he felt so connected.

To *her*.

They were inside. Leona waited. She didn't move.

"You're in shock, aren't you?" Boyd asked, closing thumb and finger around her chin, lifting it. He stared down into her face in concern.

"You know I am." She turned her eyes away from his searching regard, staring at without really seeing a large, light-filled Australian bush landscape that hung above the modern console in the entrance hall.

"I don't blame you." He dropped his hand, then took her gently by the arm. "Do you feel like something to eat? We could eat here or we could go out. I know an excellent Italian restaurant within walking distance."

She allowed him to lead her into the living room, with its double height coffered ceiling and contemporary architect-designed furniture. The total effect was one of supremely elegant individualism. Masculine, most certainly, modernistic, but welcoming to women. She knew Boyd had bought the place because of its history. This was one of Sydney's grand old dowager buildings with stunning night-time views of the city skyline. As well there were those soaring ceilings and the classic architectural elements which included marvellous fluted columns that divided the open-plan living-dining area. Architects and decorators had worked around the clock before Boyd had moved in.

"Well?" he prompted, steering her towards a custom built sofa.

"I'm not hungry."

"All the same, you should eat something. My father is a very devious complex character, but you can't let him get to you. I for one am starving. I always have a very light lunch before a match— God, it seems like years ago instead of this afternoon—nothing at all at afternoon tea, there were so many people wanting to talk to me. I need to feel *human* again."

"It was wrong of you not to tell me," she said, clutching a striped silk cushion to her breast like some kind of defence.

He sat down beside her, intensity in his blue eyes. He was wearing a plain white T-shirt and navy jeans and even then he was handsome enough to take a woman's breath away. "Tell you what?" he asked. "That my father was infatuated with your mother, who had *no* idea at all, for a brief period in their lives? What good would that have done?"

She turned on him fiercely, tears standing in her eyes. "It would have explained Rupert's attitude towards me. He's never seen me as a person in my own right. When he looks at me he sees my mother."

"We all do, Leo," Boyd pointed out gently. "For that matter, I couldn't count the number of people who've remarked on the colour and shape of *my* eyes. Everyone in the family knows I inherited my eyes from my mother."

"So some part of them does remain?" she asked more calmly.

"Definitely. Turn your head and the family see Serena. Turn your head and you'll see Blanchards, dead or alive. Every family has its own genetic blueprint."

She couldn't be consoled. "It was sick, Rupert lusting after my mother. I can't use any other word. She was a happily married woman. Besides, he had a most beautiful wife—your mother. I always knew Aunt Alexa had suffered."

"Most of us get to do our share of suffering, Leo," he said in a taut voice, taking the cushion from her and throwing it onto an armchair. "Falling in love isn't all that rational, is it? It blindsides us. Dad didn't do anything *too* terrible. He didn't go after Serena like he goes after everything he wants. He didn't break up his marriage, which evolved into little more than shadow play, or hers. My mother stayed for *me*. Much as I'm not in a mood to say it, I have to consider Dad as a victim. Falling in love with the wrong woman could be a very special hell."

"You think so?"

"I've waited a hell of a long time for you."

That filled her with real shock, then a wave of elation that quickly gave way to suspicion. "So I was being seriously considered from early on?" She didn't wait for an answer but swept on. "At some level you hate your father, don't you?"

His handsome features tightened. "No, I don't hate him, Leo," he said, putting his hand over hers. "How can I? I don't want to hate anyone. It does no good at all and he *is* my father. He's always backed me."

"Not in this!" Her breath fluttered and she drew her hand away from the surge in her blood. "Is that why you're doing it?"

He trapped her hand again, his blue eyes burning into her. "I'll forget you said that."

"*Is* it?" she persisted with a rush of emotion. "All of us can see there's great rivalry between you."

"The hell you can!" he bit off. "The rivalry is all on my father's side. I've tried as hard as I know how to be a good son, a good heir. I know Dad had a very tough time with my grandfather. There was always the constant pressure on him to measure up.

I feel pressure too, but not in the same way. I'm not at war with my heritage, which I've often felt Dad was. Rich kids, like Dad was, can suffer extreme emotional deprivation, Leo. You should know a bit about that."

"Oh, I do," she confessed, "and I wasn't even a rich kid."

"But you *are* part of the family."

"Well, being taken under the wing of a rich kid like you was riches enough for me," she said ironically. "And there's the fact that my surname *is* Blanchard."

"And it's going to remain that way," he assured her, a naturally dominant man.

She wanted nothing more in the world than to slump against him, have him gather her up. Didn't he know she basked in his strength? Love for him was beating painfully in her throat. Even then she found herself unable to break free of the cycle of confrontation. "Because you say so?" she flashed.

"Because I say so," he answered quietly.

"So it's a kind of duty to marry you, is it?" It was stupid but she couldn't seem to get control. "A bit like royalty? At least Leo knows how things work! She's not likely to rock the boat. Once the family is over the initial shock, they'll start to philosophise—well, it's not *all* that bad, is it? Tailormade in a way. Leo is, after all, one of us. She *has* shown she knows how to conduct herself.

No wild card there." She broke off the perfect mimicking. "I tell you, Boyd, this whole thing has spooked me."

"Is it any wonder?" His eyes were on the pulse that beat frantically in the hollow of her throat.

"And it can only get worse." She had seen the harshness, the massive affront in Rupert's face, and he was a man one crossed at one's peril.

"My father isn't going to fight me on this," Boyd said, sounding utterly self-assured. "But, should he try, he'll find for the first time in his life he won't win."

"*Second* time," she corrected and gave a broken laugh. "He lost out on my mother."

His eyes held an electric blue flame. "Please forget that, Leo. It was nothing more than a fantasy. What's real is this—I'm not going to lose out on *you*. I wouldn't consider it for all the money in the world."

"Nice to know then you're not going to lose any," she mocked. "I can't pretend I'm overjoyed by your very pragmatic proposal. *Deal*, I suppose we should call it. I want to keep my dignity and my sense of self intact. It's hard when I have to keep reminding myself I had to buy your silence to protect Robbie."

"Is it?" Boyd gave a brief laugh, then rose to his six foot plus. "God, I'd almost forgotten Robbie, though he did precipitate matters. Our defining moment came when I caught you red-handed with the Blanchard Diamonds."

"I gave them back, didn't I?" She still felt the panic.

"Ridiculous! You didn't take them in the first place. You love your kid brother so much you would even have taken the rap. Well, it's time for a fresh start, Leona. For you and for Robbie. He has to quit the unloved boy act and his multiple addictions. The way you always cover for him is actually hindering his self-development. I'm telling you now. I've already told him. One more foolish move from him and he's out on his ear. If I were Dad, he'd be as good as a dead man. Now, I think we should eat. You look as ravishing as ever, though a mite pale. I'll change out of this T-shirt and jeans. Give me a few minutes. We can walk to the restaurant."

They went out into the balmy night. A high sky awash with stars. They bloomed over the Harbour, as they always did over water, extravagantly beautiful diamond daisies. It seemed as if everyone in the world was in love as they made their way to the restaurant. Comfortably married couples, leaning in towards each other, strolled along the street or dipped into arcades, admiring the brightly lit, expensive speciality shops that included a society florist who charged an arm and a leg for a sheaf of long-stemmed roses. Music spilled out from somewhere. A very old favourite, but with a modern twist. Young lovers, interested only in one another, appeared unable to untwine their limbs. A family was coming at them four abreast, the youngsters clearly enjoying themselves and their night out on the town. The party split in two and fell to either side of Boyd and Leona, who smiled and thanked them.

Car lights threw streams of silver foil down the ebony surface of the road. Tail-lights glowed red; a kaleidoscope of colours from neon signs on the buildings. Traffic lights flashed red, amber, green. Busy cosmopolitan Sydney with such general goodwill in the air, Leona thought. They were looking towards Sydney Tower, one of the tallest buildings south of the equator. She had dined countless times at the Tower's revolving restaurants, which afforded arguably the most splendid panoramic view in the world. Sparkling Sydney Harbour in all its magnificence: the Harbour Bridge, the iconic Opera House with its glistening white sails, surrounded on three sides by deep blue water, the city buildings and, beyond the city central, its famous blue and gold beaches. One could see clear out to the Pacific Ocean on the one side, the mountains of the Great Dividing Range to the other. Loving her home town the way she did, Leona felt a surge of pleasure.

Delicious Italian food further soothed her. Diners sat deep in conversation, some flushed with sexual invitation, reaching across to hold hands.

She finished two glasses of an excellent red, then took the unprecedented action of asking Boyd to pour her another. She did enjoy a glass of wine, especially champagne, but she was no drinker. Rather she was discovering the numbing effects the fruity wine was having on her distress. She didn't have to drive home—*was* she going to get home? They had finished one bottle. Now they were onto another. Boyd, as ever, looked perfectly sober. She imagined she did too. But mightn't he be over the limit to drive? It didn't take much. Blanchards shunned bad publicity and Boyd was ultra responsible. Maybe he planned on sending her home in a taxi, which perversely aggrieved her. There were plenty whizzing up and down outside.

The small, beautifully shaped trees that lined this exclusive little enclave were twined with sparkling white lights. That lifted her spirits as well. She had never been to this restaurant before. She liked it. Trust Boyd to find it. The staff were unobtrusive but she realised they were being waited on hand and foot. No doubt Boyd always left a large tip.

"Feeling better?" Boyd asked. She was aware that he had been studying her right throughout the meal.

"How could I not be? This is a seriously good restaurant."

"Our secret," he said, giving her a smile that made her shiver.

She leaned forward to whisper, "It doesn't just cater to *you*, Boyd Blanchard. I'm going to bring friends here. They ought to be famous."

"Your friends?" He lifted a black brow, pleased to see she was looking happier.

"No, the chefs at this restaurant. How precisely am I getting home? Or are you going to suggest I walk?"

"I bet you could do it too." He finished his short black coffee, then lifted a hand for the bill. "How is it you look like an ethereal dream when you're so athletic?" He slanted her a mocking smile.

"I aim to be strong," she said. "I work out." She watched him add a substantial tip to the bill before handing the plate along with his platinum credit card, back to the waiter, who had appeared like a genie from a bottle.

Back out on the pavement, a good-looking young busker was moving around, violin tucked into his neck, playing the most romantic of solos. He had to be one of the Conservatorium's best students, Leona thought, because his playing was absolutely top class, thrilling really. One reason perhaps why he hadn't been moved on. A small crowd was sitting listening, and there were intermittent bursts of applause, while others continued strolling. The scintillating environment drew the crowds, day or night.

"Leave him something," Leona prompted, in

the next breath realising that Boyd had no need of a prompt.

"I usually do," Boyd told her dryly. "I'm a very generous man. Haven't you noticed?"

Once she was accidentally bumped by a slightly manic young man wearing huge yellow sunglasses, no matter it was night-time, obviously showing off to his giggling girlfriend. Boyd quickly tucked Leona in to his side. "Real catch, isn't he?"

"They're probably both at school. So do we shout for a taxi here?" She tried hard to sound composed, but she wondered if he could feel her trembling.

"My thoughts were that you should stay the night," he said.

In an instant her blood changed course. It began to whoosh madly up against her artery walls. She didn't know what was going to happen next.

"Don't have visions of my trying to seduce you," Boyd told her smoothly. "It's not going to happen. I'd just feel a lot happier if I had you in plain sight."

She felt so foolish, standing there, bereft of words. "I'm not suicidal," she managed at long last. Not suicidal, just wired inside. *Stay the night!* He wouldn't have to try a centimetre to sweep away her every last inhibition. She thought of him, pulling her to him, his hands on her, his mouth on her... Oh, God! Even the godless prayed when they were in trouble, she thought. Not that she was godless. She was definitely a believer. This was the *worst* thing and the best thing that could happen to her. She should agree right away.

"Staying over is out of the question!" she said, swallowing hard. Another minute and she would lose touch with all reality. It was a huge problem being in love with someone—at the same time making sure they didn't know it. Soul-destroying really to have to hide one's feelings from the person you loved most in all the world. But how could she make a clean breast of it when he couldn't—or wouldn't—or worst of all, didn't feel the same as she did. Love was terrible, terrible, terrible and there were many degrees of it.

"How you do go on, Leo," Boyd gently mocked her. "It seems like a very good idea to me. You've had a huge upset. Dad really can be the most callous of men."

"I have to say he is. There's such an emptiness in him. And, behind the powerful persona, a strange neediness. Jinty, on her own admission, can't fulfil his emotional requirements. Probably after we left a huge fight broke out."

Boyd gave an ironic laugh. "Jinty would have backed down fast. She surprised me when she said she had concerns about Dad's health. She's never mentioned it before."

They had paused at the junction, the traffic humming around them, predominantly luxury cars, waiting for the green light. "I thought Rupert saw Dr Morse on a regular basis?" she queried. She had a mental vision of Rupert's dusky-cheeked glare. And, behind it, to her mind, a kind of raw, unresolved grief. Rupert at the best of times wasn't a barrel of laughs, but that didn't prevent her from feeling compassion for him.

Boyd looked down at her. Her beautiful skin was lustrous as a pearl in the city's glow, her wind-tossed hair a glittering aureole around her small fine-boned face. She didn't know how beautiful she was. Her beauty, like her musical speaking voice, was simply a part of her.

"I know Dad has been taking blood pressure medication for years now," he said. "He's drinking too much these days, which would probably reduce or wipe out the effect of the medication." The light changed and they moved off as a couple, her arm linked through his. "People have stopped smoking in droves, yet Dad still goes for the Cuban cigars. I've said as much as I can say to him. He doesn't listen anyway."

"So how would you feel if he suddenly had a heart attack, God forbid?" Leona asked, feeling wretched. "Why don't you just call this whole business off? At least for now. Let him come to terms with the unacceptable, if that's at all possible. Besides, don't a lot of men think one girl is as good as the next?"

Boyd's laugh was without humour. "I'm definitely not one of them. I *won't* call it off, Leo, because it suits me very well. What's more, I refuse to talk about it further. You'll just have to be good and slip into the role of being my fiancée. It won't be difficult for a clever young woman like you. In a few months' time, we'll have the wedding. You can name the day. What about it?"

Her hand shot up as a gust of wind blew a thick skein of hair across her face. "Boyd, I can't!"

"Why not?" he asked very reasonably, helping her tuck the long lock behind her ear.

"Because…because…" Red wine soothed. It also excited the blood.

"You don't really know why not, do you?" he said.

"I do know you've set us on a very dangerous course. Your father was obviously intended by nature to be a tyrant. Maybe you will turn into a tyrant at some stage."

"It can't happen if I have you," he retorted and pulled her closer. "I can always rely on you to pull me into line. Besides, do you know anyone better you'd like to marry?" he asked, dodging an elderly man who appeared to be either dead set on walking into them or simply didn't see them.

"I haven't been thinking of marriage at all," Leona lied. "I'm more into a career, or haven't you noticed?"

A smile brushed his handsome mouth. "Leo, I know your job means a lot to you. You do it extremely well. Your job is safe. Bea has been known to frighten assistants to death but the two of you get on very well."

"Well, I'm used to frightening people."

"Tell me about it," he groaned.

They were back inside the apartment, which was more like a house. She went about switching on lights that were grouped on slim, elegant power boards. "This is some pad! We could be high up on a mountain. Far away from the world."

"Is that how you feel?" he asked in a voice that made her pulses drum.

"Leading question." She continued wandering about as though new to the penthouse when she knew it well. "It all turned out very well, didn't it? It's sort of sculptural in a way. Masculine, but female friendly."

"And it suits the purpose." He followed her, keeping a few paces away. "Personal space, business space. I can switch on or I can switch off completely."

"What are you now?" She didn't dare turn to look at him, instead running her hand over a small bronze sculpture of a horse—Tang dynasty, she knew. Both she and Boyd loved the arts of Asia.

"Bordering on the disturbed," he confessed quite unexpectedly.

She spun in shock, meeting his brilliant blue

gaze. "Isn't that the way we usually are when we're together?"

He acknowledged her point with a dry smile, beginning to shrug out of his light beige cotton jacket, worn over a blue open-necked cotton shirt. It came to her that manufacturers didn't make women's shirts in that beautiful shade of blue. She would talk to Bea about it. "Are you going to sit down?" Boyd asked.

"No, I'm going to wander," she said, moving about as though she couldn't contain her restless excitement. "You and the architect and designers worked well together. The interiors are great, both the informal and the formal. It's a reflection of you. Boyd Blanchard. Literally the Man at the Top. This has to be four or five times the size of my apartment."

Boyd settled himself into a plush sofa, spreading both arms along the back. "It's big because it has to be, Leo."

"I know that. Anyway, I love my apartment. Chloe been here? Stayed overnight?" She gave him a swift challenging glance.

"Who's Chloe? I've never heard of her!"

"I hate to say this, but *I* have. Lots of people are going to be upset if you push through with this."

"Why don't you let me worry about that?" he said. "Since you mention her, I should tell you I've said nothing whatever to Chloe that would—"

"I thought you didn't remember her?"

He ignored the jibe. "That would give her to understand that I hoped to marry her. We've known one another since we were kids."

"So in the end she was just one of the girlfriends?"

His eyes narrowed. "If I didn't know better, I'd think you were jealous."

"No way!" She shook her head emphatically, though her heart felt heavy in her breast. "Really, when I think about it, it might be best if I go on home."

"But it's pouring outside and you have no umbrella," he joked.

"Then how come I can see the stars shining?"

"Here, come and sit beside me." He patted the sofa. "We'll just talk. It's me, Boyd, remember? You're acting like you expect me to launch into wild erotic games."

"Perish the thought!" A kiss—kisses, maybe. Madness. She knew neither of them could stick to kisses. Whatever flaws there were in his grand plan, they had well and truly discovered they had chemistry to burn.

"So you can't have a worry." His manner was utterly relaxed.

She drew a slow breath. Didn't he know she was vibrating with nerves? Too much was happening to her, way too fast. The idea of their being a couple—an engaged couple—struck awe into her. She couldn't bear to think of Rupert's fantasies involvng her innocent mother. That would have to keep until later. It seemed as if Rupert had longed all his life for what he couldn't have.

"Trouble is, I'm a working girl, Boyd," she explained briskly. "I need to go home. Organise what I'm wearing tomorrow. I can't go to work, in any old thing. Bea expects me to look great at all times. It's part of the job."

"And you're known for it. Don't worry, I'll wake you early," he promised. "I have a board meeting at eight-thirty."

She shook out her glittering cloud of hair—red, gold, copper lights. "If I could only work out what you *really* want of me," she said with perplexity. "Okay, I recognise some things—"

"Tell me *what* things," he challenged.

She sheered away from that. She had the unnerving feeling that she must look as if she urgently needed to be touched. It was taking every ounce of her self-control to deny him, deny herself. Nonetheless, she found the backbone to say, "Thank you, but no. I'd like you to call me a cab."

He didn't argue. He stood up. "All right, if that's the way you want it. But I won't let you go home alone. I'll come with you and take the trip back."

"It's not necessary." She was so strung up her blood was bubbling away like streams of lava.

"I'll do it, all the same," Boyd said, every bit as determined as she.

She began to walk rather frantically towards the entrance hall, but in the end she couldn't stand it any more. She spun round quickly, unaware that Boyd was so close behind her. He loomed above her, trapping her in his blue gaze.

"Boyd!" She came close to breaking down, only her lungs were out of air.

He took hold of her as if he owned her. As if she were the very image of his every desire. "God Leona," he muttered, breathing her in. "I just can't…can't…be without you any more."

At his words, her mouth opened like a rose. She didn't want to think. She only wanted to *feel*. She had been waiting for this since for ever, suppressing every natural instinct. Now all she wanted was to let go. There was only his breath mingling with hers, his mouth, their burning need, the swift slide into the most passionate rapture that had at its centre an element of melancholy.

Love was ecstasy. It was also a force that made intolerable demands. It stripped away pretence. It stripped away all defences. She stood with her arms locked around his waist. He was cupping her face in his hands, holding it up to him. Whatever words or lack of them were between them, their physical intimacy had developed at breathtaking speed. Now it had a life and a will of its own, saturating them both in its heat.

Boyd's hand moved slowly, voluptuously, lan

guorously, down the silky column of her neck, over the slope of her shoulder to her breast. She moved even closer to him, crushing her body against him, willing his seeking hand to find the tight little bud that was her nipple. He had such beautiful hands. Thrillingly, one cupped her small high breast. She shuddered as his thumb began to move with exquisite eroticism over the aroused peak.

Excitement was soaring, beat by beat. This was to die for. This never to be borne, piercing sweetness. Sweetness the love poets spoke of so eloquently. The overwhelming flood of feeling she was experiencing was so matchless it was allowing her to dream dreams where Boyd was with her always.

Moving with ravishing slowness, he lifted her, understanding her want was as great as his. They were in the master bedroom. She was lying on the huge bed, on top of the luxurious quilted pearl-grey silk cover. He stood at the side of the bed, his lean body poised over her. "I want you here like this always," he murmured, bringing down his arms so that his palms lay flat on the bed on either side of her. "Sleep with me?"

"And let you take my soul?" He already had her body. She stared up into his sapphire eyes. This was Boyd, the man she had known and loved since she was a child. Wasn't it likely she had been programmed by the stars to fall in love with him? The splendid room seemed to be fading in and out. The high ceiling was swooping…there was only him. And her. Everyone else was far away. Her rapt state had little to do with the wine she had drunk at dinner. It had much more to do with being drunk on love. A love so powerful it could be regarded in some lights as entrapment.

"Does a woman lose her value once she sleeps with a man?" she asked very quietly.

He gave a twisted little smile. "How can you of all people ask me such a question?"

"No, Boyd. *Listen* to me." She half raised herself off the bed, clutching at his shirt front. Her beautiful eyes were filling with tears. "If we do this there can be no going back."

His expression turned tender. He lowered himself onto the bed beside her, gathering both her hands in his. "My darling Leo, the last thing I want in this world is to go back. We go forward. Everything I have. Everything I am. Everything I hope to be. I'm handing it all over to you."

The way he was looking at her, the sound of his voice, gentle and low… Not only her heart, but her whole life was in his hands.

"You belong to me, Leo," he said. " I belong to you. You never fail me."

Could he bestow a greater compliment? He looked utterly sincere. She lay back again against

he pile of silk cushions, throwing her arms above
 her head in a pose that was unconsciously erotic.

His hand fell to stroking her beautiful hair.
"Don't fight me," he begged. "Don't fight us. Not
now."

She gave a little wince of regret. "I only fight
you because I think I can't let you get the best of
me."

He bent his head to kiss her trembling mouth.
"Leo, I'll take anything you can throw at me to get
the best of you. Besides, our little spats were only
a distraction, weren't they? I suppose they served
a purpose while you were growing up. But not
now. God, what a day!" He sighed, throwing back
his dark head and momentarily closing his eyes. "I
was totally incapable of sending you home. I want
you here with me. *Finally.*" He glanced down at
her willowy body. "I want to undress you. I want
to do it right now." He spoke in such a deeply caressing voice it seemed to her she could refuse
him nothing. "Is it a safe time for you?" He leant
forward to search her eyes.

She felt her whole body flush, her answering,
"Yes," barely above her breath.

Immediately he dipped his mouth to hers, gathering her into his arms so hungrily that every last
barrier might have been removed.

"Do you realise how frightened I am?" His
ardour was so lushly powerful her very flesh

seemed to be melting. Could she really give him what he wanted? He was a deeply passionate man. Could she satisfy him as she so desperately wanted to? Could she satisfy the desire that glittered in his eyes?

There was an exquisite gentleness and under-standing in his downbent gaze, as if he read her mind. "Sweetheart, you're safer with me, more free with me, than you could be with any other man. Your well-being is more important to me than my own. My only concern is to make love to you like you deserve. So, my love, where do we start?" He reached down a hand. "With the shirt, I think. I hate these little buttons."

Her voice trembled as she tried to make a joke. "You can't rip them. This outfit was very expensive."

"And it looks it too. I love the way you dress, Leo. I love all the different ways you do your hair. I love your voice. I'm in constant awe of your charm."

It was dizzying to hear such things, although Boyd had always complimented her on her ap-pearance—really *looked* at her. She didn't mean to say it, but somehow it came out. Part of her inse-curities? "How many women have you slept with?"

His glance licked across her like a blue flame. "Suddenly I forget." Very smoothly he removed her fine cotton shirt, tossing it onto an armchair, exposing her stretch-silk bra.

"Pretty," he said, trailing a finger into her creamy cleavage. "Cheeky even, Ms Blanchard! I bet the briefs match."

"I love good lingerie." She gave a fluttery breath, passing rapidly to a rapturous excitement. Beneath his moving fingers lay her heart. It belonged as much to him as her.

"I should tell you I slept with Mark Tyler." Get it over, she thought. Create trust?

He frowned slightly. "I know."

Mortification brought the blood to her face. "You know everything, don't you?"

"Yes."

It had been her first time—she had thought long and hard about it—Mark was a tender, caring person, but in the end it had been a mistake. Afterwards she couldn't begin to imagine why people raved about sex. Her experience with Mark had been a case of reversed stereotypes. Mark had been the one in tears while she had passed very quickly to wanting him to get dressed and go on home.

But then her heart belonged elsewhere. Little detours, she had found to her cost, served no good purpose. She wanted and wanted...and the only one who could satisfy that want was Boyd.

"I once had the misfortune to be caught in a bar with poor old Mark," Boyd was saying. "I had to sit through a maudlin two hours while he mourned your split. He adored you."

"Adored me?" she gasped as he caressed her body. "Didn't take him long to get engaged. You had your affairs. By the time I was twenty I thought it high time I had mine. My two, that is. Neither of them worked. You were a curse laid on me in childhood."

He broke off his exquisite ministrations to place a silencing finger against her lips. "Leo, don't say that!"

A silent tear rolled down her cheek. "I'm sorry. I meant blessing. I really shouldn't be saying any of it. I'm no match for you, Boyd."

"Sweetheart!" There was a look of the utmost concern on his striking face. "You more than match me. I'm *mad* to make love to you, but if you don't wish it…"

Now she couldn't suppress her urgency. "Kiss me," she said, reaching up to clasp a hand around his handsome head. "Kiss me." At that moment she felt proud and strong. Maybe even a little bit in charge.

Boyd's laugh was exultant, coming from deep in his throat. "I'm going to cover you in kisses, starting at your toes. But first I think I'll finish taking off your clothes."

CHAPTER SEVEN

LEONA MADE IT TO THE office on time. She was in such a state of euphoria she had to resort to auto-pilot. It would take her days, weeks, years to fall back to earth. She wouldn't have been surprised if someone had stopped to tell her the jacket of her Gucci suit was on inside out. But no one mentioned it as she entered the lift, or as she walked through the office, although she wasn't actually walking, more like floating on air. She supposed she smiled and waved, offered little pleasantries like she always did when she came into work.

Sally, her much valued assistant finally got through to her. "Oh, good, you're here, Leo. Bea said she wanted to see you in her office the *instant* you arrive." Known for her unflappable temperament, Sally sounded fevered. Bea did tend to have that effect on people.

"Did she say what for?" Leona put her bag down on the desk.

Sally snorted. "God, Leo, Bea doesn't confide in the likes of me." Bea could, on occasions, be excruciatingly rude. "But she looked kind...kinda..." Sally tipped her nut-brown head to the side, searching for the right word.

"She looked what?" Leona put something away in a drawer, and straightened up.

"Sort of worried, unhappy, can you believe? Bea always behaves like God."

"I'll go to her," Leona said. "Do I look okay?" she asked, as Sally was still watching her.

"You look *wonderful*." Sally responded with utter sincerity, thinking that dressing was an art form that for all her efforts had somehow escaped her. Leo had such style, mixing up this and that, colours, belts, scarves, what have you, always individualising everything. She wouldn't have the courage. "All lit up from inside," she concluded.

Leona gave her the loveliest smile. "Thanks, Sal. I can't think how I got dressed this morning."

"Big night?" Sally asked, rolling her eyes.

"Something like that." The best night of her life. She'd lost count of how many times they had made love, their wants and needs had been so great. She felt she had taken Boyd in through her every pore. The more she got, the more she wanted. No sensation in the world could surpass the feeling of having him deep inside her, then coming, and coming again. This was what the great novelists wrote about and even then it was so much more.

She had desperately wanted to *feel* love, fearing it at the same time. What she'd got was the answer to every woman's prayers. But the fervour of it all had somehow weakened her knees. What she wanted was maybe a few hours' sleep...then to be awakened by Boyd, finding her reflection in his sapphire eyes.

"Sit down, Leo," Bea said, sounding oddly as if she was coming down with a cold. She was frowning too and her frown grew deeper by the minute.

"Do we have a problem?" Leona asked, intuition working overtime. She had taken to heart what Rupert had said. But surely he couldn't have made a move on her this quickly?

Bea's laugh was as brittle as cracked glass. "I've known for donkey's years you're in love with Boyd."

Leona blinked. "Can you say that again? No, never mind. How do you know—do I have a sign on my forehead?"

"Why wouldn't you be in love with Boyd?" Bea stared back at her intently. "God, come to think of it, I'm in love with him myself. We *all* are. I've never met anyone like him for all my world travels."

"So what's the matter, then? You look upset, Bea."

Bea pulled a mirror from a top drawer, held it at

arm's length, then closer. "Dear God, just as I expected! My worst fears confirmed. I swear it gets harder and harder to look presentable. Sometimes I remind myself of a garden gnome wearing haute couture. We've really bonded, haven't we, Leo?"

"We're soul mates, Bea," Leona said. "I love and admire you."

"Oh, dear!" Long regarded by everyone in the business as hard as nails, Bea made a wry little face. "Don't make me cry. No use beating about the bush, Leo. Our Lord and Master rang me last night."

"What time?"

"Does it matter?" Bea's painted eyebrows rose.

"I suppose not. Rupert wastes no time getting cracking. He wants you to give me the boot, right?"

For answer, Bea picked up a ballpoint pen and hurled it across the room. "Probably unlawful. Unfair dismissal. No, he wants me to give you a promotion."

Leona sat bolt upright. "I know! He's going to open a Blanchard flagship boutique in Outer Mongolia?"

"Close. No, he wants you to take over from Rosie Quentin at the Perth store. Rosie isn't young any more; we'd been thinking of replacing her, as it happens. Of course with a sizeable golden handshake. Rosie wouldn't go quietly into the night."

"And sending me across to the other side of the continent is Rupert's way of weaning me off Boyd. Is that it?"

"Truly you're a smart girl," Bea said, smoothing a hand over her newly pewtered bob. It would be fair to say the colour didn't suit Bea at all. Bea's former colour had been close to ebony—more in keeping with her long heavy-lidded ebony eyes—she called them currants in a doughnut, but one had to tread very carefully with Bea. "Rupert might be my boss but, just between the two of us, the man's flawed. He wants you away!" Bea threw out her short arms. "And that's an order!"

Leona gave a hollow laugh. "I couldn't care less what Rupert wants," she said and meant it. "Boyd has assured me my job is safe. *You* still want me, don't you, Bea?"

Bea frowned so fiercely her eyebrows made a straight line. "Dearest girl, surely you know I'm grooming you to take over from me. Why else have I put in all this effort?"

"And, hey, I appreciate it," Leona said. "There's no one in the business to touch you."

"Oh, a couple have tried." Bea waved the contenders away. "The truth is I'm a genius."

"No one else like you," Leona confirmed. "Let me talk to Boyd about this, Bea."

Bea gawped at her. "Dearest girl, you're not

going to come between father and son? Rupert could go into cardiac arrest if he's crossed."

"And there's *my* father," Leona said.

"Good God, so there is!" Bea reeled back. She knew Rupert Blanchard and his capacity for punishing anyone who hindered him. "You need to get your defences ready, my girl—speak to Boyd," she advised.

Leona had to wait until the Board Meeting was over. She knew from Boyd that Rupert wouldn't be in attendance. Rupert was at Brooklands. She made her way to the top floor of the Blanchard Building, the nerve centre, where she never normally went, whiling away the time by looking down on the city through the tall plate glass window while Boyd finished off a conversation with two of his father's most powerful allies, one of them Jack Compton, Chloe's father.

"Why, it's Leona!" Stewart Murray, the merchant banker who lived like a prince, still very dashing in his sixties, and with a prodigious liking for good-looking women, greeted her with open pleasure. "How are things with you, my dear?" He beamed, kissing her on both cheeks. "You look lovely. A really, really lovely girl. There's something absolutely delicious about a redhead."

"Why, thank you, Mr Murray—" Leona smiled "—I'm very well." She turned her attention to

Jack Compton who, she noticed, had gone very grey and was set to go snow white. "How are you, Mr Compton?"

"Fine, Leona," he huffed, as if Leona didn't happen to be one of his favourites. "I was just telling Boyd that Chloe will be home on Monday. We've missed her. We should all go out to dinner some time."

"That would be lovely, Mr Compton," Leona said, knowing it would never happen. Lord knew how Jack Compton would react when he learnt she had snatched his beloved daughter's intended bridegroom.

Boyd was waiting for her outside his office door. She drank him in—all the marvellous details. He was wearing an expensive suit, tailored to fit like a glove. He was so tall and lean and he carried himself so well, their top male model, internationally in demand, couldn't do better. His brilliant eyes sparkled, his whole image dynamic, glowing with health and energy in a very sensual way.

"You look beautiful," he said, his eyes moving caressingly over her. "I have to agree with Stewart. Redheads are absolutely delicious. Come into the office." He asked over his shoulder, "Everything okay? Not that I'm not thrilled to see you here."

"Listen, I have to talk to you," Leona began, shutting the door. "It's urgent!"

He was instantly alert. "I won't let you change your mind, Leo," he warned.

"It's not that."

"Then nothing else matters," Boyd said, attempting to draw her into his arms.

"No, Boyd!" She drew back. "You've got to hear this. I'm very worried that Rupert might take his anger out on Dad. Dad could lose his job or get shifted, even demoted." Her father was still relatively young, he could find another job, but none she was sure, to measure up with the pay and prestige of Blanchards.

Boyd made a little clicking sound of impatience. "I thought we'd agreed I'd handle this."

"Yes, but Bea spoke to me this morning. Rupert rang her last night. Rosie Quentin—she's in charge of Fashion in Perth—is due for the chop. Rupert wants me to take over."

"Have you gone mad?" Boyd locked his hands around her willowy waist, drawing her to him and not letting her get away.

"It's not me!" she protested. "It's your father. I mean, Perth's a great city. I love Western Australia—"

Boyd silenced her with a kiss. She returned it. How could she not? She could have kissed him for ever. "I'll speak to Dad," he said.

She put her hands on his shoulders, staring into his beautiful eyes. "Chloe's father suggested we should all go out to dinner. Can you believe it? They'll be totally unprepared."

"How could they be totally unprepared?" he said crisply. "I've told you—"

"I know what you told me. I believe you."

"Why, thank you." He gave a wry smile.

"But people can and do believe their fondest hopes will be achieved. Instead of bolstering the Compton hopes, Rupert should have been shooting them down."

Boyd's laugh was a shade impatient. "Odd, that! Dad does get a great kick out of raising people's hopes, *then* shooting them down. Leave it to me, Leo."

What else could she do?

It turned out to be a hectic day. Bea couldn't see a thing right with the glossies from the latest fashion shoot. She swished the photographs—excellent really—off the table in a fit of frustration. The models, male and female, the glorious North Queensland tropical location, the clothes they were wearing—everything met with scathing contempt. Bea had conveniently forgotten she had hand picked the lot.

"I've got it!" Leona found herself interceding at one point, just about ready to try anything. Shots in the local cemetery? Maybe the fire station? Would that capture Bea's attention? "Take them all out on location to Uluru. The contrast between the beautiful sophisticated clothes and the savagely beautiful Outback environment could be brilliant."

Lights flicked on behind Bea's dark obsidian eyes. "Now why on earth didn't *I* think of that?" Suddenly she was happy. "Well, well, what are you waiting for?" She clapped her hands together, then waved Leona off. "Go and find me Daniel."

Later on Leona rang Robbie to check that he would still be going with her to the airport to meet their parents, who were due in from Hong King early the following morning.

"I don't understand why you want me," Robbie said, genuinely puzzled. "Your dad has only said half a dozen sentences to me in all the time he and Mother have been married."

"Well, it's not as if he's excessively jolly with me," Leona reminded him. "Anyway, saves me hanging around by myself. So set your alarm."

"Actually, I might stay up all night instead of going to bed," Robbie suggested.

"Not if you want to look your best. Besides, I've got something to tell you."

"Something good, I hope." There was a sudden note of anxiety in Robbie's bantering tone.

"Might as well tell you now. Rupert wants to call a halt to any wedding plans. He and Boyd had *words*."

"Fantastic!" Robbie's voice carolled loudly

down the wires. "Wish I'd been there. Don't worry about old Rupe, Leo. Boyd is already long strides ahead of him. If I were you, I'd start planning my wedding gown. Something utterly exquisite and a veil with a long train. Two little flower girls, maybe a pageboy, if the kids will consent to do it these days. After all, the whole continent will be watching. It's actually thrilling and of course I'll be a groomsman." A reflective pause. "You're not thinking of breaking my heart, are you?"

"Never!" Leona said stoutly.

"A true blue Blanchard can be best man," Robbie said generously. "I'll be for ever in Boyd's debt. Honestly, he deserves some kind of medal. He's got those thugs off my back. Unbelievable, I'm *safe*! I can come out of hiding!"

"Make sure it stays that way," Leona warned with enough firmness to register.

Robbie's answer rang with sincerity. "I swear to you, Leo, I'll never place another bet. I've learned my lesson. I could have ended up in a police line-up—probably their best-looking ever suspect—instead I received mercy and a second chance. All I want to do now is earn the respect and trust of the people who love me—you and Boyd. Well, you, anyway. Boyd might learn to love me as I make a clean sweep of all my bad habits. After all, I'm going to be godfather to your first child. Or one of the godfathers. I could live with that. And there's another thing," he confided. "I plan on visiting Italy in the summer vacation. It's just possible I might get to see my dad."

In a nerve-racking day Leona found herself smiling with satisfaction. "You've made the right decision, Robbie," she said. It could well be that Delia had been holding back on her son for many long years. Delia was like a lot of other women who fancied themselves wronged, and may well have had her revenge on the wrong male.

Although her father and Delia knew they were being met, their faces registered neither pleasure nor appreciation.

"Surely you have morning lectures, Roberto." Delia lost no time getting underway, her voice set at that familiar grinding edge.

"Not until eleven, Mother!" Robbie retaliated by giving his mother a great big bear hug.

"Oh—oh, be careful!" Delia cried, wrenching herself away. Robbie had come perilously close to messing her hair, a glamorous cast-iron coiffure regularly tinted a champagne-blonde. It was a style she hadn't changed in years.

"You needn't have bothered, Leona," her father was saying, accepting her kiss on his cheek with no visible sign of emotion. "We could have caught a taxi home."

"No bother, Dad." Leona kept her smile in place

when she felt like seizing her father by the arms and shaking some life into him. Her father, though a handsome, quietly distinguished-looking man, bore little resemblance to the happy, loving father she remembered from her early childhood. It was as though the real Paul Blanchard had died with her mother. Emotionally speaking, he gave every appearance of a man who had lost all feeling. "Marital frostbite", Robbie called it. "Mother does a super job of that!"

"Goodness, we might have to hire an extra car for all the luggage," Robbie observed as they jostled with the crowd at the baggage carousel. Delia was busy pointing out a number of pieces of designer luggage as they came tumbling through the shute. "I expect you've brought lots home for me and Leo, eh, Mother? Clothes, leather goods, Swiss watches."

"Oh, do stop, Roberto," Delia chastised him. "I mean, what *else* could you possibly want?"

"What about a return ticket to Rome?"

Delia turned on him in what looked like shock. "Why Rome?"

"Why not?" He leaned forward to grab yet another bag. "I think it's high time I met my dad. Remember him, Mother? Carlo D'Angelo. The last time I saw him, he was making a run out of our house with you chucking things at him, missing every time."

"Shut up about that, Robbie, right now!" Delia said angrily "Your father was a sorry specimen of humanity. He left us both." All of a sudden Delia, normally a picture of health, was looking quite sickly.

"Shall we go?" Paul Blanchard actually took action. He seized hold of his wife's arm. "People are looking, Delia," he said in a warning undertone. "We can't have that. If Robbie wants to meet up with his father again, neither of us have the right to stop him."

Robbie looked momentarily gobsmacked, then he indulged in a triumphant high-fisted salute picked up from the local champion tennis player. Delia could rage non-stop for seven days and seven nights but she wouldn't stop her son from making that trip, Leona thought. Carlo D'Angelo may have bolted from his first marriage but there remained the distinct possibility that he hadn't forgotten his first-born child.

"Would you like me to make tea or coffee?" Leona asked some ten or fifteen minutes after they had arrived at her father's and Delia's house. Large, modern, architect-designed, it was impressive with a great location, but mercifully not overly pretentious.

Robbie had already left. "I'm outta here!" he'd told Leona in a quick aside. Even so, he was looking happier and more in charge of himself than she had ever seen him.

"God, no!" Delia responded graciously. "I want my bed. I detest that last leg of the flight home."

Leona looked to her father. "I wonder if I might have a word, Dad?"

Delia laughed as though Leona had said something utterly unreasonable. "Not *now*, Leona. Your father is as jet lagged as I am. I would have thought that was obvious."

"Actually, I feel perfectly well," Paul Blanchard answered in his usual courteous manner. "What is it you want to speak to me about, Leona?"

"It's private, Dad," she said. The last person she needed was Delia right under her nose.

"Really?" Delia gave a vehement shake of her head. So lavishly had it been sprayed, not a single hair moved. "Does that mean you don't want me?"

"I wouldn't keep you from your bed, Delia," Leona said very sweetly. "You do look a little peaky. Would *you* like some tea, Dad?"

"I suppose I would." He suddenly gave her a smile—that rare smile that caught at her heartstrings. "You look very beautiful, Leona. What's been happening to you?"

"Why don't we go into the kitchen?" Leona said and moved to take her father's arm. "I'll make the tea and I can tell you then."

But there was worse to come.

"You and Boyd?" Paul Blanchard sat at the long

bench in the very sleek contemporary kitchen, eyeing his daughter with genuine shock.

Not a good sign, but Leona felt she had to meet the challenge.

"Yes, Dad. Me and Boyd," she confirmed quietly. "He wants to marry me, even though it appears it's come as a tremendous shock to you."

Paul Blanchard was driven to resting his dark head with its silver wings in his two hands. "But Leona, we all know Rupert's plans." He lifted his head again. "The Compton girl. It's almost a business deal. That's the way Rupert's mind works. Unite two dynasties. Rupert and Compton have been waiting for the relationship to deepen. I thought you understood that."

"I did," Leona answered, frowning. "But you can't seriously believe Boyd is going to allow his father to pick his bride for him. You *know* Boyd. It's preposterous. He's his own man."

"Leona, I'm well aware of that." Paul Blanchard sighed deeply. "I think the world of Boyd. We all do. It's not a question of Boyd having to measure up to his father like Rupert had to measure up to his, and incidentally never did, which I believe seriously affected Rupert's character. The Old Man watched Rupert's every step like a hawk. He even had his spies. On the whole, Rupert had a rough time. But, that aside, Boyd is ready right now to take over Blanchards. What's more, the majority of the

Board will back him. It's another case of the King and the Crown Prince. I can almost feel sorry for Rupert. His resentments remain deeply entrenched. This news of yours will precipitate a huge rift between father and son. It will affect Blanchards, the whole family. That's what you're telling me isn't it? Rupert is totally against you and Boyd."

Leona studied the leaves at the bottom of her teacup as though they held the answer. "I think you could say that. Rupert is used to riding roughshod over everyone. He's trying it out on his own son. It won't work."

"No, it won't," Paul Blanchard agreed. "But the more Rupert thinks about it, the worse things will get. The man's a tyrant. My dear, even *you* have no idea. Rupert has become more and more power drunk as the years have gone on. He could hurt me, you know, not that I wouldn't survive. So don't worry about that. But we're *all* vulnerable where Rupert is concerned."

"Do you think Rupert would actually stoop to manoeuvring you out?" she asked worriedly.

"In the blink of an eye," Paul Blanchard confirmed, mercifully not sounding all that worried about the prospect "The man is heartless. I know in one way he is enormously proud of Boyd, but in another he recognises his son has qualities he never had. Rupert is into power for power's sake. Boyd isn't like that. He's a very different human being. That's his mother in him. Wonderful woman, Alexa. She made a terrible mistake marrying Rupert, but then again they were manipulated by the Old Man. To be very, very rich, Leona, is something to be avoided. Great wealth ironically doesn't bring happiness. It brings terrible risks. You might remember that. If you marry Boyd, your whole life will change. You're my daughter. I love you. I'm afraid for you."

Leona could see her father was deeply serious. "Don't be afraid, Dad," she said. "I know I can trust Boyd with my life. There is something I would like to ask you. Did you ever feel at any time that Rupert was a bit too fond of Mummy?"

Her father turned to look at her as though she had said something utterly crazy. "What in the world put that idea into your head?"

She gave him an imploring look from her beautiful green eyes. "Just something Rupert himself said. I mean, I was as shocked as you, but lots of people have something to hide, Dad. I think Rupert's secret was that at some stage he became infatuated with my mother." Tears sprang unbidden into her eyes.

"Darling girl," Paul Blanchard groaned as he reached to put a hand on her shoulder. "If Rupert the old bastard, was ever infatuated with my beloved Serena he forgot to tell *us* about it. I never saw anything of the kind. And I can put your mind entirely at rest regarding your mother. She had absolutely no idea. Why, Serena and Alexa were great friends! They loved one another. Your mother loved me. I never did know *why* she did, but she did. We were wonderfully happy, the three of us. Either Rupert is a total liar, delusional, or he managed to keep this perverted infatuation very well hidden. The thing is, Leona, *everyone* loved your mother. She was immensely lovable. My love for her has never faded. Only a small part of me is still alive. I know you can see that. The best of me went with your mother."

Leona took her father's hand and held it. "Do you see too much of her in me?" she asked sadly. "Do you, Dad? Please tell me."

Now tears stood in her father's eyes. "I've hurt you a lot, Leo. I beg your understanding and forgiveness. But you're right. You're so like your mother, a lot of the time the pain becomes unbearable. It's what's known as good old-fashioned despair."

"Yet you married Delia?"

Paul Blanchard's broad brow wrinkled. "I married Delia because I thought she would have the generosity of spirit to become a surrogate mother to you. I saw things in her that apparently weren't there. My own fault. I wasn't seeing straight at the time. I was like a man in a coma. I should have known, just seeing how Delia was with her own little son. Roberto has suffered as well and he didn't deserve it any more than you."

"I'm afraid that's true, Dad. But surely it can all change; it's not too late, even for you. Robbie told you he wants to go in search of his father."

"Then I'll give him all the help he needs. It's possible he might find out a great deal that his mother has never wanted him to know. Delia became very warped after Carlo left her. I know Carlo loved his boy. I do know that. Roberto is the very image of him. Part of Delia's policy was to keep Carlo out of his son's life. It's an alarming thought, but Delia could easily have kept so much from Roberto."

"I've been thinking along those lines myself," Leona admitted. "Do you feel you and Delia should stay together, Dad?" she asked after a minute. It was her fervent belief that her father and Delia would be better apart.

Paul Blanchard gave his daughter a twisted smile. "I can't find it in my heart to talk to her about a divorce."

"Maybe it's what you both need," Leona said. "At the very least, you can bring things out into the open."

"You mean a kind of purge? It would be pretty awful to divorce Delia, Leo."

"She deserves a good shake up," Leona said.

Her father gave a sad laugh. "I have to agree with that. But it's not us I'm worried about at the moment. It's you and Boyd. Rupert can be a very menacing man. He thinks nothing of hurting people. He'd better make sure he does nothing to hurt you, my darling, or he might get what he thoroughly deserves."

The *my darling* from a father not given to endearments nearly brought Leona to tears.

CHAPTER EIGHT

LEONA WAS WALKING briskly to her car in the basement car park, humming a little melody she had made up on the spot. Something romantic. She had a flair for such things. She was having dinner with Boyd that night and the familiar excitement had started up in her blood. For the first time she allowed herself to believe he might *truly* love her as a man loved the woman he wanted to marry. What had happened with Robbie had nothing to do with anything. The incident with the earrings had merely been an excuse, a blind, Boyd loved her, she knew it. Maybe she had always known it. The thought exhilarated her right down to her toes.

"Leona!" a peremptory voice called. "Don't drive away. I want to speak to you."

Leona spun round, infuriated by the tone of voice and the presence in the basement of its owner. "Well, I don't want to speak to you, Tonya," she said sharply. "What on earth are you doing here? I have to be somewhere else. Boyd and I are going out to dinner."

Tonya's rather spindly legs covered the short distance between them in record time. Strangely, she kept shaking her left foot as though a pebble had lodged in her high heeled sandal. "Why do you think he's decided to marry you and not Chloe?"

It was spoken with such extraordinary venom that Leona drew back a pace. "Jinty been speaking to you, has she?" Well why not? They were sisters. Even so she was surprised at Jinty's lack of discretion.

"Not Jinty, no." Tonya's sharp features tightened. "The fact is my sister and I have had a huge falling out."

"I'm not surprised. You have all the tact of a blunderbuss."

Tonya drew her mouth inwards. "Don't worry about me, thank you very much. I'm fine. It's you who should be worrying. Never mind who told me, but I *know*."

"So you want to offer congratulations?" Leona spoke very dryly.

"He doesn't love gorgeous little you," Tonya fired up. "He's *fond* of you. We all know that. But fondness is quite a different thing. You're family. He's known you since you were a little kid. But he doesn't love you as a man should love the woman he's going to marry. I mean

you're not on equal terms, if you know what
mean."

"And you've figured that out all by yourself
have you?" Leona forced herself to remain calm
when she was feeling under siege.

Tonya gave a bitter smile. "I've had inside help,"
she confided. "Not for the first time either. Every
family has a gossip and I've learned a hell of a lo
from her. Let's face it, you're suitable enough, pre
sentable, you know the score. Rupert wants Chloe
of course, but quite a few of the family have grown
tired of Rupert and his wants. They're looking to
Boyd to head up the family and Blanchards. Boyd
has chosen you for what I'm sure are excellen
reasons by his light. I've already suggested a
couple. Boyd really thinks things through. Chloe
can't hold a candle to you in looks and Boyd ap
preciates beautiful women. It wouldn't be a huge
problem taking you to bed. Best of all, you're
young enough for him to mould any way he wants.
What amazes me is how you can't see any of this."

Leona took her car keys out of her handbag
then zapped the remote. "Have you quite
finished?" she asked coldly. She really detested
Tonya.

Tonya clicked her tongue. "I know it's absurd
After all, I don't like you, but in a way I'm disap
pointed in you, Leona. I thought you had more
backbone. But you're utterly spineless. You're

eing manipulated. Can't you see that? Boyd may
e everything a woman wants—I mean even *I*
vasn't immune to his appeal—but I wouldn't trust
im any more than I would trust his old man. It
night well be you're simply a pawn in the father-
on power play. Plenty of precedence for that. And
here's that other business."

It was a clever trick and Leona fell for it. "What
ther business?" she asked in a disgusted voice.

"God, so uppity already!" Tonya crowed.
'You're not Mrs Boyd Blanchard yet, pet. And it
night never happen so don't get too carried away.
'm talking about your dear sweet mother, the
ovely Serena."

For a non-violent person, Leona felt a surpris-
ng amount of anger starting to roar inside her. It
urned, then singed. She wanted nothing more
han to smack Tonya across her sneering mouth.
'I'd stop now if I were you," she warned, her
merald eyes lit by little flames.

But Tonya was never one to heed a warning.
'Rupert had the hots for her, I've been told," she
ontinued blithely on, eaten up by malice.

Be careful, the voice inside Leona's head strenu-
usly urged. *Keep in control. Control is always
ewarded.* She was a Blanchard. She couldn't
fford to get into a cat fight.

"The same source?" she managed crisply. "A
voman as malicious as you? I think I know who

it is, but Rupert won't thank either of you fo
putting that one about."

Tonya shrugged. "What could he do? It's th
truth."

Leona by this time was feeling ill. "You have
nasty tongue, Tonya. You relish spreading dishar
mony."

"What if it was Geraldine who told me
Geraldine, Rupert's own sister?" Tonya's thin fac
took on a truly foxy expression.

*The one thing you can't do is lose it! Get in th
car. Drive away.*

To hide her feelings of immense shock, Leon
averted her head, leaning forward to open the ca
door.

"People love to gossip, Leona," Tonya taunte
her, absolutely brazen in her stance. "Even tha
arrogant old bitch, Geraldine."

Leona was severely tempted to send Tony
sprawling. Instead, she turned back to confront th
bitter, hostile woman. "Geraldine would neve
betray the family," she said with absolute certainty
"And Geraldine would never, under *any* circum
stances, confide in *you*, Tonya. You see, peopl
don't like you. They don't trust you. And with
good reason. They know just how much damag
you like to inflict."

"Such loyalty!" Tonya hissed. "But Geraldin
did speak to me. Why don't you ask her? She'l

deny it, of course, but I had to get it from *some-where*. Think now. Isn't Geraldine the most likely person? I dare you to ask her."

"I wouldn't dream of upsetting her," Leona replied, very forcefully for her. "You really are a horrible woman."

Tonya laughed, as though she thought Leona incredibly naïve. "Have it your own way, you poor deluded girl. No skin off my nose. Boyd will gobble you up, but one day he'll spit you out."

The moment she arrived home, agitated and upset, she called Boyd. He hadn't arrived home but she left a message claiming she had a headache and could they please postpone dinner?

Fifteen minutes later he called her. "I'm coming over right away," he said, firmness and authority vibrating down the line. "I know you too well, Leo. You may have a headache—I'm sorry for that—but my guess is you've come into contact with someone out to hurt you."

"That's not it at all!" Hurriedly, she tried to deny it. "There's no need to come."

"I'm leaving now," Boyd said, his tone implying that he was wise in the way of women.

In her bedroom she changed quickly from her work clothes into a loose yellow dress. Boyd always did see through her excuses. So what was she going to tell him? The last thing she wanted

to do was cause more trouble. But trouble was
coming. She could smell it. She could even put a
name to it. *Crisis.*

I won't marry you. I can't.

He wouldn't listen to that. Protests were in vain.
Never mind the fact that losing him would kill her.
Was that just another underlying fear? That one
day he might abandon her, just as Tonya had pro-
phesied? It would be bliss to live without fear, but
fear was part of being human. It wasn't easy either
accepting the fact that ultimately she stood alone.
Inside her own skin. She wasn't by nature a clinger.
She couldn't cling to Boyd.

What else might she say to him?

*Tonya claims—she waylaid me in the car park—
she and Gerri had a conversation regarding Rupert
and his infatuation with my mother.*

He would be as sceptical as she was. They both
knew that Gerri had repeatedly dismissed Tonya as
a foolish malicious woman, which she undoubt-
edly was—Geraldine seldom got anything wrong.

*What about the power play between you and
Rupert?*

Hadn't she, herself, suggested to Boyd that he
might be using her as a pawn? Hadn't he stated
his position?

Was that the real motivating factor? Was Boyd's
main focus wresting Blanchards from his father?
Boyd was extremely ambitious, with all that went

ith it. Choosing the right wife was a serious
usiness. Chloe, Rupert's favourite, didn't suit.
ut Leona, now, was suitable to take on as a wife.
was simply an extension of their early days. He
ad always taken care of her. She was part of his
orld. Moreover, he now had the knowledge that
ney were sexually compatible.

Venom, once injected into the system, was hard
o fight off. People like Tonya didn't live by the
ules of common decency. She was a sick woman
ho went around trying to spoil things for others.
he realisation came to Leona—Tonya had a fes-
ering envy for all the Blanchards. It could be a
ery corrupting thing to be drawn into the world
f the very rich, not being able to keep up with the
ace and, as a consequence, becoming deeply re-
entful of the perceived inequities in life.

oyd made no attempt at small talk. "What's
rong?" he asked, so attuned to her that he was in-
antly alert. "Come and sit down." He drew her
nto the living room, settling them on a sofa.

Then he waited.

"Well?" He took hold of her hand, studying her
orcelain profile, so strikingly offset by her flame
f hair. She was wearing yellow, a sun colour
nat he loved on her. "Nothing is so bad you can't
ell me," he said. "Nothing is so bad I can't fix it
or you."

Leona couldn't look at him. To look at him wa to lose herself. Extreme as it might sound, it wa the truth. At odd times over the last six or seve years she had dreamed of him falling in love wit her. But it had been a fantasy, her *dream*. Now h had actually asked her to marry him. The drean had come true, but with all the capacity for confli that entailed. There was an entire family, a busines empire involved here.

"Leo, I can't force it out of you," he sai gently. "Tell me."

She turned her pretty hands palms up. They wer almost imperceptibly trembling. "Where do I start'.

"Why not with the name of the person yo bumped into today? I didn't say this was going be easy, Leo. Dad has always tried to run people lives. He's tried to threaten us but it won't worl I've reached the stage where I have my own pow base. I won't give you up."

She turned to him with a faintly melanchol look on her face. There were so few people wh experienced a grand passion in life. So *few* peopl Surely she had been blessed? But wasn't Boy talking more like a man ready to seize power an assume the throne than a man deeply in love? H was used to power. It fitted him like a glove.

"Why not?" she asked plaintively.

He lifted her hand, then kissed her fingertip one by one. "Because you utterly enchant me."

"You don't seek to own me?" She was on the verge of tears. Boyd wanting to marry her, and marry her very soon, would be dizzying for any girl. Hadn't she believed, along with just about everyone else, that he and Chloe Compton would eventually make a match of it? Still, people talked a lot. Often they got it wrong. Geraldine definitely hadn't believed it. Geraldine was much older, far wiser, than she was. Geraldine was very perceptive.

"That works both ways," Boyd was saying, holding back a long curling swathe of her hair. "I own you. You own me. You're mine. I'm yours. I wouldn't knock it if I were you. The way we mesh is the stuff of fiction. The two of us together will be right at the heart of the family. If life is a journey, then I've chosen you as my life's partner every inch of the way."

"You don't see me as a blank canvas?" She wished she could stop these pathetic questions, but she couldn't. Was she, as Tonya had suggested, a young woman he thought he could mould as he wished? Ordinarily, she was far from being a pushover but there was no question who of the two of them was the dominant personality. Boyd knew it. She knew it.

"To be painted in at will? Don't be ridiculous, Leo," he scoffed. "You don't need me to tell you how gifted you are. You're so clear-sighted about

so many things, yet you constantly questio
yourself. Or, more to the point, me!" He caught he
chin, turned her face, kissed her mouth. There wa
something vaguely punishing in it, yet it had th
power to reverberate deep within her. It was
mind-bending feeling to love someone so muc
that it was almost a grief.

Closing her eyes, she asked, "Do you think tha
under any circumstances Gerri would speak t
another member of the family about Rupert's in
fatuation with my mother?"

She got an answer immediately. "Leo, look at me.

It was an order and she obeyed, meeting the ful
force of his hot blue gaze. "She's spoken to m
about it," he said. "Geraldine is my aunt, a big pa
of my life. She knew I would find out at som
stage. What she didn't know was my mother ha
already told me. One or two of the older member
of the family might have had an idea. But it's nc
a topic for discussion, as you can well imagine
Everyone was a lot closer in those days. Peopl
have eyes. Anyway, it's all in the past, Leo."

"But the past is never past, is it? It never reall
goes away. It has a habit of resurfacing when w
least expect it. It affects our behaviour. It makes u
feel good about ourselves, or it can make us fee
worthless. Why do you think I've always been s
supportive of Robbie? He desperately needed hel
with a mother like Delia."

"And you gave it to him."

"And he gave you *me,* didn't he? Isn't this what it's all about?"

"A form of blackmail?" He cocked an eyebrow at her, almost amused. "You can't *really* believe that. You're just tormenting yourself. Robbie's stupidity just brought things to a head. I was sick of the games we played, Leo. It's just as I told you. I wanted to move forward. As for Dad! Is it a crime to fall in love with someone at any age, even if that love is unrequited? I've thought so much about this over the years. You're right. The past is never over. Incidentally, there have been quite a few sexual infidelities in our holier than holy family, as far as that goes. I used to be very angry with my father, mostly on account of my mother. Now I believe that so far as Serena was concerned, Dad didn't do anything that wrong. When Cupid aims his arrows, there's not much anyone can do about it. Dad couldn't help his feelings. He's always been a soul in torment. Maybe it was part of a mid-life crisis. It's a well documented phenomenon. The point is, ultimately he didn't act on it. Feelings are one thing. We can't help them. Actions another. Actions we *can* prevent. So what are you sitting here mulling over, Leona? Obviously something has badly distressed you and I very much want to know what it is."

She was having a lot of trouble telling him.

Why? Because he didn't say, *I love you...love you...love you...*

He *did* love her. She knew that. But perhaps no in the way she desperately wanted.

Maybe the fault lay in her. Was she expecting too much? The truth was that she wanted him to lov her to bits. Why didn't she say, for that matter *You're everything I want and love. I adore you* She'd had so little affection after her mother ha died. Her father, so remote. Delia, appallingl stingy with even a kind word. Children from dys functional homes carried a lot of baggage int adult life. It seemed she was one of them.

Neither of them, for that matter, was using th L word. It was killing her.

"It wasn't that muckraker, Tonya, was it, by an chance?" Boyd was questioning with quick impa tience. "Now there's a woman who should see good psychiatrist. She's eaten up with envy of he sister. Of anyone, in fact, who has something sh so desperately desires. Was it Tonya who was lyin in wait for you? That's her style."

Leona drew a deep breath. Should she reliev her own stress and, as a consequence, make mor trouble? She didn't think so. Tonya was such fool she didn't know what she was getting into i she made an enemy of Boyd.

"So she was," he said flatly, so attuned to her h was reading her body language.

"I don't believe I said that." She was hopeless.
A bundle of nerves.

"I can read your mind."

"The blank canvas?"

"I told you to stop that."

A head rush of excitement as Boyd, with a desire
so fierce and palpable she couldn't miss it, pulled
her across his knees, a featherweight in a soft as
silk yellow dress that left her throat and arms bare
and rode up over her knees to her satin thighs. "I
won't have you trying to put distance between us,
Leo," he said, pressing her head back over his arm.
"I won't let you. Gerri would never confide family
matters to Tonya."

"I know, I know." Her voice sounded small and
contrite. "I'm sorry." A pause, then, with a flash of
spirit, "What am I sorry for?"

"I can't think of a damned thing." Boyd laughed,
a flash of white against bronzed skin. It totally oblit-
erated the daunting expression that had darkened
his face. "You're so beautiful." His hands were
moving compulsively over her, the magic of it pene-
trating her slender, streamlined body. One hand
palmed her breast, registering her rapid heartbeat.
"I want to make love to you until you don't care
about anyone or anything but me. You're mine, Leo,
but you have to trust me. That's an order. So obey!"

Who could argue? Certainly not with desire.
Who could stand fast when it swept all before it?

When his mouth came down on hers it opened like a poppy to the sun. Her breath fluttered, joined with his. To be with him was like a waking dream. A delirium of the senses. A rapture that lifted her so high she might have had wings.

They were lying in some blissful fugue state, locked in each other's arms, Leona crushed to his body with one strong arm. Their lovemaking had been gloriously passionate, both of them losing themselves in a storm of emotion. Yet it had all been soundless, save for the moans of pleasure that the flesh of one gave the other. Whatever might befall them, their coupling had the perfection one could only dream of. Was everything else just a waste of words? Leona wondered as she lay in the tender aftermath of their passion. Surely it had been ordained they should share a destiny? Where else could she find a man to love like she loved Boyd? She had to let malice and Rupert's machinations bounce off her. She had to be strong and capable. Put away her fears. Show courage. Tackle life head on. If she lost Boyd, for whatever reason, she would have to live with terrible regret for the rest of her life.

The shrilling of the bedside phone brought them swiftly back to earth. *Go away,* Leona wanted to cry to the real world but the real world surely wouldn't.

"Don't answer it," Boyd echoed her thoughts, as instinctively she turned away.

"It's all right. Whoever it is, I'll cut it short." She swung her slender legs off the bed, then picked up the handset. "Hello?" She groped behind her for the sheet, but Boyd pulled it gently away, spreading his hand over the naked curve of her back.

"Leo, is that you?"

Oh, my God! Here it comes. How many times in life was happiness overtaken by unforeseen disaster?

Beset by premonition, Leo turned her head to Boyd, one hand covering the mouthpiece. "It's Jinty!" she whispered, the pupils of her green eyes dilated with anxiety.

Boyd sat up immediately, revealing his splendid naked torso, the white bed sheet wrapped around his long legs, black brows knotting.

"Yes, Jinty," Leona spoke into the phone. "Is everything all right?" *It can't be.* Jinty rarely rang her.

"Far from it." Jinty's voice was so taut it had to be stretched to its limits. "Is Boyd with you? It's Boyd I want."

It's Boyd I want. Obviously in the scheme of things she didn't count.

Boyd, who was pressed up close to Leona so he could clearly hear Jinty's voice, put out his hand for the phone. "It's Boyd, Jinty," he said in a strong, rather clipped tone after Leona passed it over. "What's happened?"

Swiftly Leona rose from the bed to slip into her robe, fastening the sash. She didn't need anyone to tell her something was really wrong. It could

only be Rupert. Was he dying—dead? There were
always consequences for one's actions. For a
moment she thought she might faint.

"And where is Dad?" Boyd was asking. His tone
was grave, but calm. That put the strength back into
Leona's limbs.

"Come home, Boyd," was Jinty's reply.

"Well?" Leona asked after Boyd put down the phone.

"Dad has had a bad turn," he said, "or so Jinty
tells me. Dr Morse is with him."

"Is he going to be hospitalised?" Leona put a
hand to her throat, wondering if it was all her fault.

Boyd had no difficulty reading her transparent
expression. "Don't go feeling guilty, Leo," he cautioned. "Dad's not going to die. If there were something really wrong Drew would have admitted him
to hospital like a shot. What Dad wants to do is
block us any way he can. I *know* him. The worst
part of it is he's prepared to drag you into it, despite
the fact that he gave every appearance of loving
you right up until now."

"You're saying it's a ploy?" she asked incredulously. "Surely he wouldn't do that. It's so—"

"*Unfair* is the kindest word at my disposal.
Despicable might be closer. *Pitiful* closer yet.
Nevertheless, he is my father and Jinty has asked
me to go to Brooklands right away."

"She sounded so strange…frightened," Leona
said, ever ready to show compassion.

Boyd gave a cynical half smile. "The only thing Jinty would be frightened about is losing her position in life. She worked flat out to bag Dad, the billionaire. She got him and she's paid a price. They're not close, Leo. You know that. Even if Jinty had been a lovely woman—lovely inside and out, like my mother—Dad wouldn't have let her in. That's the way he is. He doesn't love anyone. He doesn't trust anyone. It must be like being in prison."

Leona shook her head in negation. "He loves *you*, Boyd."

"Only as an extension of himself," Boyd said, harshness in his voice. "And maybe only until I'd reached full maturity and shown I wasn't prepared to act on his every command. There's such a duality in him and there are many degrees of loving."

"Well, he doesn't want a bar of *me*," she whispered. "Not now!"

Boyd went to her, gathering her to his powerful lean frame. "Because at heart he's so deeply envious, Leona, and he can't combat that terrible feeling. It's the cause of the schism between us. You don't have to be a genius to figure that out. Dad has come to believe he missed out on everything he wanted. He hinted at it repeatedly, yet he hides his insecurities behind aggression. He can't bear to think *I* might get to know all that love is, when *he* missed out. Dad is not a paradigm of the virtues, I'm afraid. Dad's a tyrant; he's spent a lifetime threatening people. He must have decided early that was the way to go. He would have been happy enough to see me marry a woman I didn't love rather than let me have you."

He kissed the top of her head, then dropped his hands to her shoulders. "Come, let's take a shower together. Then we'll drive to Brooklands. It won't take long. No, Leo, don't back away. Brooklands is my home as much as his. You're with me. That's the way it's going to be. I won't have you pushed aside. Actually, I thought we might get married on your birthday, which will make you a beautiful Easter bride. What more could a man want? There's not a lot of time, but time enough to make all our plans."

Moments before they left her apartment, Boyd put a staying hand on her shoulder. "Here, I want you to wear this." From his tone he might have been suggesting she don a cardigan against the cool evening air.

"What is it? I'm warm enough. I'm—" She didn't finish. How was it possible for her to find words? Boyd had taken a ring from the inside breast pocket of his jacket.

And such a ring!

The central stone was a magnificent emerald, the colour of such extraordinary intensity it had to be

Colombian. The emerald was flanked by a blaze of diamonds that continued around the band.

"Come here to me." He swept her into his arms, showing both strength and tenderness. "If you don't like it, we'll change it."

She went to speak but her voice had disappeared. She was stunned. At the same time her sense of alarm persisted, Rupert at the heart of it. Yet Boyd was her rock. It would be Rupert who would back down. Rupert who would need to change his stance.

"I thought it had to be an emerald with your eyes," Boyd was saying, cupping her cheek in the palm of his hand. "Don't be afraid to trust me, Leo," he said in a deeply moving voice. "Don't be afraid to love me. I'm here to help you stretch your wings. Give me your hand, sweetheart. They're the prettiest hands I've ever seen." He bent and very gently kissed the sweet curves of her mouth.

"How long have you had this?" she whispered as he slipped the exquisite engagement ring down over her finger. The fit was perfect.

"Oh, I've been keeping it safe," he assured her, giving her his beautiful white smile. "Safe for *you*. Now we'd better get going. I need to talk to Drew Morse before he leaves. If Dad has had a real turn it might galvanise him into changing his lifestyle. He can't continue to disregard his health any longer."

* * *

When they arrived a couple of hours later the huge house was ablaze with lights, which Boyd found excessive. "So much for global warming," he said tersely, pulling in alongside Drew Morse's car, then switching off the ignition. "It can't be all that bad with Dad," he said. "Drew is still here, but he wouldn't leave until I arrived."

"Do you think I should stay in the car?" Leona suggested. She wasn't one to willingly cause pain. "If Rupert really isn't well, mightn't the mere sight of me exacerbate his condition?"

"You're not forgetting you're my fiancée, are you?" Boyd stared across at her. "No, you're not staying in the car. You're coming into the house with me. A house that one day will be yours. I know your tender heart, Leo, but believe me when I say Dad has planned this. It's simply a case of Rupert Blanchard pursuing his strategies. At the very least he'll think he brought a stay of action. Come along, Flower Face. We're in this together."

Jinty was waiting for them, dressed in a floor-length glamorous house gown, with a fantastic print. Her dismayed expression—she didn't have time to hide it—gave them a clear indication that she hadn't been expecting Leona. Just Boyd.

"Thank God you're here!" she cried, reaching out to grab hold of Boyd's arm. "I've nearly been out of my mind with worry."

Boyd looked at her, handsome face impassive. "Dad's upstairs?" he asked.

"Yes, his bedroom." Jinty gestured with her hand. "Drew is with him."

"So Drew saw no necessity to have Dad airlifted to hospital?" Boyd asked, still looking Jinty in the eye.

"Well…well…he was just waiting to see."

"See what, Jinty? This is me you're talking to. I don't like to sound unsympathetic, but we both know it's much more a case of Dad cracking the whip than anything else. We'll go up."

Jinty looked alarmed. "Surely it would be better if Leona stayed downstairs with me?" she asked sharply. "Rupert has been extremely upset. This might make him worse."

Boyd's frown deepened.

"Really I think you should go up on your own, Boyd," Leona advised, laying her hand on his arm. "Make sure first what condition your father is in. I'll stay with Jinty for now."

"If Dad's okay he can say hello to my fiancée," Boyd announced crisply, his blue eyes on fire.

"Check on him first," Leona cautioned. "Do it for me."

He paused, looking down at her. "Okay," he said gently.

"Come into the drawing room." Jinty drew Leona hastily away as Boyd mounted the staircase. "My goodness, I must say Boyd works fast.

That's quite an engagement ring you're wearing May I see it?"

Leona felt strangely reluctant to show her. Jinty had never demonstrated any genuine friendship towards her. She held her hand out briefly, the lights from the chandeliers flashing off the brilliant stones.

"Heavens, it's glorious!" Jinty said. "That emerald has to be—"

"Green for my eyes," Leona supplied, chopping off Jinty's estimate of how many carats there were in the large emerald and surrounding diamonds.

"May I try it on?" Jinty asked, not even bothering to fight off her lust for magnificent jewellery.

Leona found that distasteful, even shocking. So much for Jinty's being out of her mind with worry. She was still staring bug-eyed at the ring.

"It wouldn't fit you, Jinty," Leona said, gently shaking her head. "Could you please tell me exactly what *is* wrong with Rupert? As you pointed out, he's not looking after himself."

There was a hard glint in Jinty's eyes. "True, but my dear, I thought you knew what's really wrong with him. Rupert is very much against this engagement. Given that, as his wife, I don't feel I can stand against him on this. Or even remain neutral."

"So you've changed your tune?" Leona asked with remarkable composure. Jinty was having a hard time hiding her jealousy. "There've been many times you've disagreed with Rupert. I have no wish to be unpleasant, Jinty, but let's face it, it's really none of your business. Even Rupert goes way too far thinking he can dictate to Boyd. He certainly can't choose his bride. Boyd has chosen me. End of story. It would be a very good idea if you would show your usual good sense and accept that. We thought you had. Or that's what you gave us to understand. By the way, I had a run in with your sister today. She really should see a psychiatrist. It's fashionable these days."

Jinty's good-looking face registered both shock and anger. "I told that stupid creature to keep well away."

"Now that was always a tall order. Tonya doesn't listen to anyone. Do you happen to know the name of the mole in the family? There is one."

Jinty eyed her with marked dislike. "I'm sure I don't know what you mean," she said, oozing self-righteousness.

"The insider Tonya has sought information from?" Leona prompted. "I'm not suggesting it was you. Someone not averse to letting the family skeletons out of the cupboard and so forth?"

Jinty's eyes flashed with sudden recognition.

"You've thought of someone?" Was she now going to deny it?

"What do you want to know for, Leo?"

"I want to stop that person from doing any more talking," Leona said, realising that was exactly

what she intended to do. "Rather I do it than Boyd
I know you're finding it hard to deal with—I know
you've got a soft spot for Boyd—who could blame
you?—but I'm not the pushover you think, Jinty."

"No, you're not," Jinty agreed wearily, as if un
willing to carry the discussion any further. "I neve
thought you were. Young maybe, but highly intel
ligent and often very kind. The informer in the
family would have to be Frances Blanchard. She'
as sharp as a tack and a great gossip. I used to see
Frances and Tonya with their heads together. My
bet is Frances. When women aren't loved they tend
to grow bitter."

Upstairs in the master bedroom suite, Boyd shook
hands with his father's long time physician and
friend, then approached the bed. "I see you've been
giving yourself hell, Dad." Boyd turned his dark
head. "What do you reckon is the matter with him
Drew?" he asked.

Drew Morse discarded the last remnants of mis
placed loyalty to his patient. "I won't pretend with
you, Boyd. You're far too clever. Rupert here i
very much against your marrying Leona. God
knows why. I think she has to be one of the mos
delightful young women on the planet. He's been
working himself up into what one would diagnos
in a child as a major tantrum. I've told him that
Spot of tachycardia. I've taken care of that. Ruper
hasn't been looking after himself properly fo

years. The cigars have to go. Less of the fine food and drink. The after dinner brandies. A bit more exercise is in order, the usual thing. Your father is fit enough, even though he's been disregarding my best advice for years. He can do it no longer. I've told him if he doesn't he's a prime candidate for a heart attack or a stroke."

Boyd turned back to his strangely silent father, taking the hand that lay on the coverlet. "Do you hear that, Dad?"

A black shadow crossed Rupert Blanchard's heavy handsome face. He shook off Boyd's hand, then pointed a finger at Drew Morse, much in the manner of pointing a gun. "Thanks a lot, Drew. For everything. You can go now. That's my formal dismissal. Don't come back."

"Very well, Rupert," Drew Morse responded, picking up his bag. He had served Rupert Blanchard faithfully for many long years but he had always known it would come to this.

Boyd stood up for a moment. "If you wouldn't mind waiting downstairs for me, Drew," he said with quick empathy for the older man's feelings, "I'd like to have a word with you. I know you've been devoted to my father's best interests in all these long years."

Drew Morse gave a faint smile. "I'll wait if you want me to, Boyd."

* * *

"Now isn't that too touching," Rupert Blanchard sneered as the doctor closed the bedroom door quietly behind him. "Sure he gave me his best attention and he got well paid for it. I'd say attending to me alone bought him the fancy car he has outside. I hope you've come by yourself." He shot his son an intent, piercing glance.

Boyd remained standing. "Leona, my fiancée, is downstairs."

For a moment Boyd thought his father was about to spring out of the bed. "Don't do this, Dad," he warned. "It needn't be this way. Think of your own health if you can think of nothing else. The last thing I want is for you to drive yourself into a heart attack."

Rupert Blanchard shot his son a malignant look. "Sure about that?"

"Absolutely!" Boyd said in a voice charged with pity for his father but dismay for his father's mind set.

"Could I see Leona for a few minutes?" Rupert abruptly changed tack. His voice, big and blustery a moment before, went whispery with sudden weakness.

"Certainly!" Boyd agreed, his own tone softening. "As long as you give me your word you'll say nothing to upset her. She certainly won't be wanting to upset you. Leona, as we both know, has a tender loving heart."

"I know that. Just bring her up." Rupert waved

a listless hand. "You have my promise. Then you can go away. I need to speak to Leona privately."

Three heads turned towards Boyd as he walked into the drawing room. Drew Morse was sitting with the women and went to stand up at Boyd's approach. Boyd waved him back into his armchair. "That's fine, Drew. I won't be long." He spoke directly to Leona. "Dad wants to have a word with you, Leo. He's promised he'll say nothing to upset you but, Dad being Dad, I don't trust him."

Leona went quickly towards him, embracing him. Behind the composure she could see the high level of strain. "I can handle it, Boyd. Is he all right? Dr Morse says he is." Relief had settled on her lovely young face.

Boyd found he couldn't answer. "I don't want you to see him on your own," he said doggedly.

Jinty broke in. "For God's sake, Boyd, what could he do? You and Leona are engaged. Like it or not, Rupert will have to accept that. He's far from being a fool. Perhaps he's already accepted it and wants to tell Leona so."

"I'll go up." Leona made the swift decision. "Rupert used to have a lot of affection for me. Perhaps some of it has returned."

"As you wish—" Boyd sighed "—but I'll wait right outside."

"You surely can't think Rupert would harm Leona?" Jinty asked in amazement.

"He'd better not try." Boyd's answer was taut enough to cut rope.

Drew Morse shook his head. "I've given him a sedative, Boyd. That's keeping him quiet."

Boyd sat in one of the antique chairs that were dotted along the wide corridor. His body, Leona could see, was on high alert. "I'll get this over quickly," Leona said, dropping a kiss on his cheek. "I'm not a little girl, Boyd. I can look after myself."

"The slightest sign of trouble and you get out of there," Boyd said. "I'm right outside the door. You tell him that."

When she thought about it afterwards, Leona wondered how it hadn't occurred to her before.

"Please shut the door after you," Rupert requested, quietly lying back against the pillows. He looked pallid and drawn and she knew a sharp pang of pity.

"How are you feeling, Rupert?" She approached the bed and took the chair beside it.

"Groggy," he said, his eyes lingering on her though not really seeing *her* at all. "I don't think there's been a single day I haven't thought about your mother," he suddenly confessed. "The way her life ended here on Brooklands. I often go to the place. I loved Alexa passionately when I married her, but I lost her early. She quickly came to see behind the façade, to see the real me. That was the problem. She saw me for what I am. Serena didn't. She was such a lovely innocent young creature. You could be her double. All I know is in my mid-forties I fell madly in love with her. I wasn't receiving any love from my wife. I wasn't giving any either. I knew it was insane but I couldn't prevent it. I was like a raw teenager in romantic agony. God knows what would have happened, only she was killed."

"Nothing would have happened, Rupert," Leona assured him. "My mother was unaware of your feelings. She loved my father. She loved me. She loved Alexa, your wife. You did nothing wrong. Try to set your mind at rest instead of tormenting yourself with what would never have been. People constantly fall in love with the wrong person. It happens every day and every day it brings pain. Love is a mystery, isn't it? It's granted to some. Not to others. I'm so sorry your life got so twisted."

"My life—or much of it—has been utterly barren," Rupert maintained, appearing to grow angry.

"You might blame yourself, Rupert," Leona bravely suggested. "You should have cast off your bitterness, been more expansive, opened yourself up to others. You have a splendid son. That in itself is a wonderful thing. The promise of grandchildren. Instead, you've nurtured your torment. You've lived on the dark side."

He gave a grunt of bitter laughter. "Are you saying I don't have a chance at redemption?"

Leona shook her head. "I'm not saying that at all. You have every chance if you want it. We all want it for you."

Rupert stared deeply into her eyes. Not *her* eyes. Leona was painfully aware of it. Rupert had never seen her for herself.

"I'm no saint," he told her harshly.

"No, you're not," she agreed. "Neither am I. I try to do my best."

Rupert didn't hesitate. "How much would it take for you to go away? To break off this engagement? You can give Boyd some cock and bull sob story. You don't think you can live the lifestyle. He knows exactly how difficult it is. But I've been thinking. Everyone wants money. I'm prepared to give you a lot."

Leona felt any residual feeling she had for Rupert sink into the mud. "Wouldn't I be getting a lot as Boyd's wife?" she asked, assuming a Jinty inspired world-weary tone.

For a moment Rupert looked bitterly disappointed in her, then he said, "Is that why you're marrying him?"

"Of course." She nodded her red-gold head. How long she could sustain this act she didn't know.

Rupert sat up in the bed. "What a wonderful actress you are," he rasped with massive contempt. "Perfect performances. So go on then, name a figure. Might as well. My son won't be ousting me just yet, my girl. I'm good for another fifteen to twenty years. I'll do the right things and I'll have the best of care. So how much will it take to make you happy?"

Leona lifted her left hand to stare down at her glorious ring. "How many stars do you suppose are in the Milky Way, Rupert?" she asked. "I read once it was around one hundred thousand million, same number as our brain cells, though you appear to have lost a few million of those." Abruptly she stood up. "Boyd, very sadly, is quite right. Incredible as it may seem, you want to deny him happiness. You know he'll find it with me. I adore him. I always did. First love. Last love. Only love."

"Bitch! You bitch!" Rupert cried out, falling back against the pillows.

Leona walked very calmly to the door. "Goodnight, Rupert," was all she said.

CHAPTER NINE

TALK OF THE RIFT between father and son spread lik
a summer bush fire. Everyone in the two Sydne
stores got together in groups, wondering and whis
pering about what might happen. Through all th
years Rupert Blanchard had been the bogeyman, th
boss who struck terror into the staff. Some of ther
had dreadful memories of him stripping pieces o
them. Boyd, thank the Lord, was entirely differen
The new wave Blanchard, enormously popular wit
the staff. They were behind him to a man. H
already had the female vote. Leona was easil
accepted as a great, if surprising choice. No one ha
picked up on the big romance. The two of them ha
been extremely quiet about it.

Leona openly wore her ring, accepting a neve
ending flow of good wishes from near and fa
which for the most part were utterly sincere.

Robbie had been exuberant with joy. "You'r
really, really meant for each other."

Geraldine had put it a little differently. "About me!"

"Gosh!" Sally sighed when Leona showed her the ring. "You have to be the luckiest girl in the whole wide world!"

"And Boyd is the luckiest man!" Leona retorted, then they both broke into laughter.

"Seriously, you're the perfect couple!" Sally pronounced when she sobered. "Bea says she knew it was going to happen from way back. Yet she never said a word."

"Pays not to," Leona warned.

Two days after Chloe Compton arrived home from New Zealand, she rang Leona asking her if they could meet for coffee. Chloe had received phone calls when she was in Auckland, telling her to come back as soon as she could—something was wrong. The one thing Chloe hadn't counted on was losing Boyd to his cousin—or cousin of sorts—Leona Blanchard. Everything she had seen had given her to understand the two were antagonistic. Well, not exactly *antagonistic,* but that was as far as she could get. They were always sparring anyway.

Leona's first instinct had been to drop the phone, instead she thought furiously as Chloe was speaking. Meeting Chloe didn't seem like a good idea, especially as Chloe couldn't manage her best wishes or at a pinch congratulations when every-

one else around Leona was doing so. She didn
think she could bear Chloe telling her how broker
hearted she was, drowning them both in misery. I
the end she told Chloe she was all booked up for
least a fortnight.

"Maybe I could come to your apartment on
evening after work," Chloe suggested. "I promis
I won't keep you long."

"You know where I live?" Leona asked i
surprise. With her Blanchard name, she liked t
keep as anonymous as possible—even her tele
phone number was ex-directory.

"Of course," Chloe responded, uncharacterist
cally sharp. "Boyd pointed out the building to m
one evening when we were driving home fror
dinner. From recollection, I think he said, 'That
where my little cousin lives'."

Leona found that impossible to believe. Apa
from anything else, Boyd would have to have gor
right out of his way to drive past the buildin;
"Maybe you're mistaken about that, Chloe," sh
said, maintaining a friendly voice. "Boyd has nev
referred to me as his little cousin, even when I w*
little. Can you tell me over the phone what this
all about? I can understand and I sympathise if yo
got it wrong about Boyd's feelings for yo
Probably we can't be friends right now, Chloe, bi
in time?"

Chloe hung up on her.

* * *

Chloe announced herself at the apartment the very same evening. Obviously she knew Boyd was in Melbourne for a few days.

"Could I come up, Leona?" she asked, standing squarely in front of the video screen so Leona could see her.

How could she refuse? Chloe was a respectable young woman from an establishment family. It seemed very unkind, even unmannerly to refuse her entry. Not without misgivings, Leona pushed the button to release the security door. Why was Chloe so desperate to see her? Was she about to tell her she and Boyd had actually talked marriage?

That couldn't be. Just *couldn't*. So many things were happening in her life, she felt pounded to a pulp.

Chloe duly arrived at her door, a tall angular young woman, attractive without being eye-catching, good dark hair, chocolate-brown eyes, always beautifully dressed. Her fine skin was blotched with colour. "I'm sorry about this, Leona," she apologised, "but I have to talk to you." She stepped into the apartment before Leona could even move away from the front door.

"Well, come in," Leona invited wryly. "Can I offer you something—tea, coffee, a stiff drink?" Actually she didn't have any stiff drinks on hand. Some white wine and beer in the fridge was probably the best she could do.

"White wine, if you have it," Chloe said,

slumping onto one of the living room sofas. "Thi
is such a mess!"

"I hope you don't mean the apartment." Leon
tried for a little lightness.

"God, no, it's lovely. Just like you." Chloe's voic
was faintly trembling. "I mean what's happened."

Leona stood there, facing the other youn
woman. "You surely can't mean our engagement?

Chloe began to cry.

"Oh, please don't cry, Chloe," Leona begged
"Here, I'll get you something to drink."

Swiftly she retreated to the galley kitchen t
pour them both a glass of wine. *A mess? Okay, let
think*. The worst possible scenario—and it *di*
happen frequently in real life—was Chloe about
confound her by telling her she was pregnant wit
Boyd's child?

Get a grip. Boyd had told her to trust him. Tru
him she would.

Chloe left off drying her eyes. She accepted h
drink, then took a hearty gulp. "Are you reall
certain Boyd is the right man for you, Leona?
she questioned.

Leona bit her tongue against a sharp answer. "
couldn't be happier, Chloe." Calmly she took
seat on the sofa opposite.

Chloe placed her hands on her hot cheeks. "Wh
wouldn't you be?" she moaned. "You've landed
great prize. It's the very opposite for me. Th

arents, especially my father, are in a terrible state.
t's like a bomb has been dropped on them."

"That seems very extreme," Leona said. "I know
ll the talk was of an alliance between you and
Boyd, an arranged marriage in the good old tradi-
ion, but that's what it was, Chloe. *Talk.*
Misinformation put about by Boyd's father and
our father. We both know they're the kind of men
who love running their children's lives."

"Fathers!" Chloe said bitterly, downing what
ittle was left of her wine. Leona thought it inad-
isable to offer her another. "Do you know, for the
irst time in my life Daddy was actually paying me
ome attention," she said, earning a big twinge of
ympathy from Leona. "He'd hoped for a son and
e got me. If I'd been a fish he would have thrown
ne back. I've been miserably conscious I'm a
othing person since I was a child. Do you under-
tand that, Leona?" She shot Leona an appealing
gonised glance.

"I do and I'm *so* sorry, Chloe." Leona felt
enuine pity for the other woman.

"My big chance was to land Boyd," Chloe
onfided. "That would have made me really
omeone in Daddy's eyes."

"Maybe you and Daddy set your sights too
igh?" Leona suggested. "Women have been
hasing Boyd since he left school."

Chloe was biting her lip with tension. "Why

wouldn't they?" she said. "He's a man to take
woman's breath away. I love Boyd. We've know
one another since we were children. I was prett
sure he was falling in love with me."

Leona had been prepared for this so it didn
come as the blow that perhaps was intended
"Could you swear to that, Chloe?" she asked. "
know Boyd, the man. I'm certain he wouldn't hav
given you false hope."

"We went lots of places together." Chloe lifte
her chin. "Daddy thought it was a very good sig
Rupert always made a fuss of me, singled me ou
You must know you're currently in high disfavour
Rupert is absolutely furious with Boyd."

"None of which will do you any good, Chloe
Leona was becoming tired of this whole convers
tion. She glanced at her wrist watch, giving a littl
start. "I don't like to hurry you, but I'm dining ou
this evening." She had no difficulty telling the whi
lie.

"But Boyd's in Melbourne!" Chloe huffed, a
though that was the first step in Leona's journe
to becoming unfaithful.

"I do have friends, Chloe," Leona answere
mildly enough. "Now, if there's nothing else I ca
help you with?"

Chloe stood up, squaring her shoulders an
gathering her very expensive designer ba;
"Daddy will never forgive me for losing out o

oyd," she said. "It was my one opportunity in
e to gain his approval."

"I'm sure there will be others," Leona replied
ntly. "Why don't you try to make a life for
ourself, Chloe? Moving out of your parents'
ome would be a start."

Chloe looked back at Leona with startled eyes.
And lose out on my inheritance?" she cried.
orry, that's just not on!"

So much for independence!

fter Chloe left Leona was overtaken by a strange
neliness. Women in love were so terribly vul-
rable. What she desperately needed was Boyd's
assuring presence.

At nine-thirty the phone rang.

She flew to it. "Hi, Flower Face. I've been tied
 in meetings all day. Couldn't wait to ring
ou…"

In an instant all Leona's doubts and fears were
own away.

hey were back in place the following day.
mmediately she caught sight of Boyd's face
eona knew something had gone terribly wrong.
e had arrived back from Melbourne mid-after-
on. They had dinner planned for this evening.
ow he had arrived at the apartment, looking so
azingly handsome, so formidable, the sheer

maleness of him made her reel. It was almost as a big argument was on simmer, waiting to boil.

"Is something wrong?" she asked, eyeing hi tentatively. He hadn't kissed her. Was it a wonder she felt a black cloud descending?

"Why didn't you tell me Dad offered you mon to break off the engagement, leave town, overseas?" he asked, a muscle working along th clean-cut line of his jaw.

She stared back at him, speechless.

"No answer?" he asked, his blue eyes brillia with high mettle.

Was she going to have to live with this for eve

"Who told you?" she countered. She had nev said a word to Boyd about her last conversatic with his father. It was too demeaning, not to her b to Rupert. Loving Boyd like she did, she wasn about to offer him further upset. Now it seem that had been a tactical error. The Blanchards dea in tactics, didn't they?

"Okay, so it's true." He pulled her to hir locking an arm around her. "What was the fin figure?"

She leaned back against his arm. Fiery sparks electricity. "What did Rupert tell you?" Becau she was so stung, she spoke in a provocati manner quite unlike her.

"Ten million." His tone was tight with disgus

She broke away with a brittle laugh, moving in

he living room. "Pretty cheap, I'd say. You're worth
ar more than that, Boyd." Her tone was unmis-
akably contemptuous. "I'm holding out for more."

He came after her, fighting down his explosive
nood. He'd had a tough agenda and he was nearly
ead on his feet. "You won't get it or anything like
," he said. "I don't believe a bloody word of it
nyway. Why didn't you tell me? Why *won't* you
rust me, Leo? What can I offer you that will make
ou love me?"

She spun so quickly the skirt of her lovely sea-
reen dress swirled about her legs. "I do love you!"
he was swept by passionate revolt. "But you're a
readful lot, you Blanchards. You're famous for
•eing dreadful. There should be warning placards
aying: Don't get mixed up with this lot! You want
o know what's going on? I'll tell you. Chloe
Compton arrived on my doorstep yesterday, des-
•erate to unburden herself."

Boyd groaned aloud. "You didn't tell me that
ither."

"I didn't want to upset you," she answered hotly.
Now I simply don't care. Your horrible father did
ffer to buy me off. I didn't tell you because I
nought it too demeaning to Rupert. Shows what I
now about how low Rupert can stoop. As for
Chloe, she accepts you don't love her—"

"Love her? God!" Boyd's expression indicated
he level of his disgust was sky-high. "Go on. She

told you we were lovers. We were trying to have [a]
child together. I'm prepared to believe anything[.]
He threw his tall elegant body into an armchair.

"She didn't go that far," Leona told him coldl[y.]
"Poor Chloe considers herself a nothing perso[n.]
Landing you would have been the definin[g]
moment of her life. Her father would have bee[n]
proud of her for the very first time."

"Being proud of his only daughter—his onl[y]
child—is a problem for Compton," Boyd sai[d,]
gritting his fine teeth. "Why doesn't Chloe have th[e]
guts to get out and make a life of her own[?]
Anyway, forget Chloe. Sad for her, she *is* forget[-]
table."

"I think even she realises that. Anyway, I thin[k]
Chloe believes—maybe a lot of people do—yo[u]
and Rupert are fighting a duel with me in th[e]
middle."

Boyd groaned, thrusting a frustrated han[d]
through his crow-black hair. "That's probably tru[e.]
We *are* fighting a duel. But it's not one *I* broug[ht]
on. I'm content to succeed my father in due cours[e.]
This isn't about me or you, Leo. It's about Dad. It[']s
about how life has warped him."

"So it's a fight to the finish?" she asked, breath[-]
ing fast. There was so much emotion in the roo[m]
it was draining the air out.

"I won't give you up, Leo," he said. "Not f[or]
Dad. Not for Blanchards. Not even for *you*. Are w[e]

going out to dinner, or are we just going to go to bed?" he asked, an unbearably cynical note in his voice.

At his tone Leona angrily pulled the pins out of her beautiful hair and shook it free of its arrangement. "Neither, as it turns out," she said in the manner of a young woman who had had enough. "I don't give a damn about going to bed. This has gone right beyond sex. I won't be used as a pawn, Boyd. I'm a *woman!*"

"My God, aren't you!" he said, getting up and coming towards her. He didn't want half measures. His whole being was crying out for her.

"Don't you dare kiss me!" she threatened, tears standing in her eyes. "You didn't kiss me when you arrived!" she accused him, every word ringing with intense disappointment.

Boyd took her face between his hands, bringing it closer to his. "Well, I'm kissing you now." He bent his head and began to kiss her passionately, like a drowning man clinging to his one hope in life.

"Come to bed with me, Leo," he whispered between the most ardent of kisses.

"I won't. I mean it," she cried, her small fists clenched hard. It suddenly seemed immensely important to stand firm. She fought off the familiar waves of desire that were flooding her body. Besides, there was this strange exhilaration in

defying him. No matter how much pain she wa
giving herself, she had her pride. Did he love h
or lust for her? Was she the silly sacrificial lamb

"Okay!" Abruptly, Boyd threw up his arms in a
exaggerated movement of surrender. "I don't kno
what else I have to do, Leo. Right now, I'm s
bloody tired, I'm fresh out of ideas. I want you s
badly I can hardly think of anything else. But I'
not going to tolerate your switching on and off. I'
not going to tolerate your keeping things from me
I understand your motives, but I think you woul
know I can handle any amount of upset. It's th
keeping things from me I don't like. I've asked yc
to share my life. Doesn't that say it all? You're no
some bimbo I lust after. Give me a break. Eithe
we're together or we're *not* together. It's up t
you."

The ultimatum delivered, Boyd turned on h
heel and strode to the door.

Within seconds her hot raging blood ran cold i
her veins. She had to fight the powerful urge to ru
after him, but her thoughts were all over the plac
In the end she let him go, even though he was a
inseparable part of her. She had to think this whol
thing through. Not only Rupert was trying to driv
them apart. It took her a while to realise she wa
crying silently, the tears sliding down her cheek
Boyd was prepared to stand up to his father, th
most ruthless of men. Rupert couldn't control the

ives. Why was she so afraid? Even her father wasn't afraid that Rupert might ruin his career with Blanchards. He was prepared to move on. Possibly without Delia at his side.

What, then, should *she* do? She sat down on the sofa with a box of tissues, folding her legs under her. The surest way to wreck her life was to lose Boyd. He was so much stronger than she was. More equipped by nature and long experience to cope with all this fallout. What she had to do was face up to the demanding job of becoming his wife. Probably if she were a few years older she might be able to cope better. It hadn't been easy being part of the Blanchard family. But she did owe them a lot. Most of them, as she had so recently found out, were right on side with her. All except the most powerful Blanchard of them all.

Either we're together or we're not!

Boyd had challenged her and with good reason. She had to let go of her fears. It wasn't Rupert who could destroy her dreams.

She realised with a sense of shock it was *her own self.*

An hour later she rang Boyd at his apartment, judging he would have had ample time to arrive home. She was all ready with her apologies, desperate to make up. What woman in her right mind would risk losing such an extraordinary man? She

wasn't going to have to walk through life alone
She had Boyd.

The phone rang out and his answering service
picked up. He hadn't gone home.

She did her best not to break down. She left he
message. *"It's me. I'm so sorry for tonight.*
don't know what gets into me at times. Speak to
you tomorrow."

It was as much as she could manage without dis
solving into a flood of tears.

Leona was not to know it, but Boyd had gone ove
to his aunt Geraldine, his long time confidante and
supporter, to talk through the dark situation hi
father—her brother—had mired them in. They
talked until so late that Geraldine suggested he
stay the night, which he did and not for the firs
time. Geraldine now knew the full story but she
would never say a word. Nevertheless she had been
ready with plenty of advice.

"Nothing wrong with a man speaking his mind,"
she said. "But you have to remember Leo's age and
her tender heart. Then there's the fact she's being
beset on all sides. Drat that Chloe. She needs to ge
herself sorted. Rupert has been responsible fo
such a lot of hurt. No need to tell you that. You'l
be seeing Leo today, of course."

"Of course." Boyd bent to kiss his aunt's cheek

* * *

As it happened Boyd had outside appointments for most of the morning so Leona wasn't able to get through to him.

"I'll tell him you called the moment he arrives, Miss Blanchard," said Vera Matthews, his secretary. Although Leona had often invited Vera to call her Leona, Vera, a woman of the old school, immensely capable and loyal, stuck to the more formal Miss Blanchard.

She still hadn't heard from Boyd by lunchtime so she went off in search of a solitary coffee. She had asked Sally to join her but she was so snowed under she said she would have a bite to eat at her desk.

It was as Leona was returning to the office just under an hour later that she saw Rupert and one of the Blanchard Board members in intense discussion outside Stewart Murray's merchant bank. She couldn't do as she wished and cross the street to avoid them. She couldn't get caught jaywalking on top of everything else.

It was Bob Martin who first spotted her, smiling and tipping the brim of his hat. Bob was a nice man. Rupert was at work again; no doubt he would be looking to ensure Bob's support if any battle was to take place in future. She smiled back, pointing to her watch and quickening her step, miming that she was late back for work. She could have gone over but she couldn't bring herself to do it. She was disgusted with Rupert. She was trying

very hard not to be frightened. Rupert was such a
intimidating man. Yet men like Rupert had a
absolute certainty that they were always in th
right.

The pavements were thronged with people
workers coming off or going on their lunch break
tourists, shoppers clutching lots of bags. She wasn
aware of Rupert until he spoke from directly behin
her. "You know exactly what you want, don't you
my dear?" His tone was deliberately low but sh
heard every grim word with unnatural clarity.

"Yes, I do, Rupert," she said quietly with clear
headed courage. Her strength had returned. Sh
turned to face him as he came alongside her, a bi
handsome man, faultlessly groomed, with
palpable aura of power and, it had to be admitted
on this day of days, a frightening aura of violence
"I want your son. I want Boyd. He knows exactl
what he wants too. The best thing for us all, Ruper
is to be family. The worst thing would be for yo
to enter into a losing battle with Boyd. He doesn
want that. Neither do I."

Rupert's eyes narrowed to slits and his cheek
flushed red. "Such insolence!" He gave a hars
laugh.

"Please, Rupert," she begged, feeling sadnes
for the man he had become. The worst part wa
that it seemed impossible for him to change.

They were now close to the junction, facin

Blanchards' main store, hemmed in by the lunch-time crowd. Leona had never felt so uneasy in her life. Yet her own personal safety wasn't on her mind. The opposing traffic was given the green light at the precise moment that a brutally strong hand moved to shove her in the middle of the back. She let out a cry, closing her eyes as her willowy body, unprepared for the onslaught, bowed forward. She lost balance in her high heels and tumbled onto the road.

People nearby reacted in an instant, filled with alarm, but frozen in position. It was all happening so fast. Others hurrying to catch the lights wondered what was going on. The young woman with the beautiful mane of red-gold hair appeared to have catapulted from the pavement into the direct path of the oncoming cars. One skidded around a corner, avoiding certain trouble. The following car, an SUV unaware of the woman in the road came on. No city driver dared to hold up the steady stream of traffic. A woman with her small daughter standing to the left of where Leona had been standing cried out, terrified.

Leona herself scarcely had time to panic, though she expected to be run over in the next moment. Only Rupert galvanised himself. He scooped her up from behind, all but flinging her slender body back into the crowd without thought for himself and the dangerous proximity of the oncoming

SUV. The driver, however, was swiftly to realise in
horror that he was going to hit a pedestrian
No comfort at all in the fact that the pedestrian
shouldn't have been on the road with the lights
against him.

Rupert's tall heavy body was picked up and
flung down on the road as if he were no weight at
all.

The whole world seemed to grind to a stop and
Leona fainted for the first time in her life.

The six o'clock news started with a bulletin
Rupert Blanchard dead—although the shocking
news had already broken on the street and on the
Internet. With sombre faces and subdued voices
anchor men on different television channels
relayed the account of how the retail giant, bil
lionaire and philanthropist, one of the richest men
in the country, had bravely put his own life on the
line to save that of his future daughter-in-law
Leona Blanchard, who had recently become
engaged to the Blanchard heir, Boyd Blanchard
Rupert Blanchard had been swiftly transferred
from the accident scene to the nearest hospital but
tragically he had died en route from a fatal head
injury.

Leona, still in shock and detained at the hospital
almost believed it. Rupert had given his life to save
her? Let everyone believe it. At the end he did. The

est was best left unsaid. She had given a statement to the police. She had told them she felt dizzy and had stumbled in her high heels. Rupert had been here when he was desperately needed. The tragedy was that he had been unable to save himself. She would never forget his sacrifice.

That would be the family line. She *was* family. Boyd was now at its head. Responsibility had already fallen heavily on her shoulders. She could bear it. Rupert had punished himself in his own way.

"A terrible, terrible thing!" the young nurse in her room said, tears standing in her eyes, her voice very gentle. "He must have loved you a great deal."

It had taken hours for Boyd to take charge of what was now a tremendous crisis for Blanchards. More was expected of him than most other people. He had grown up with that. Staff all over the building were crying, a sure indication that great wealth alone was enough to bring forth tears, he thought with faint bitterness. His father had not been loved.

Boyd had spoken to everyone he wanted to speak to, needed to speak to. He had given endless instructions thanking God for his personal staff's cool, calm efficiency in the midst of chaos. All he wanted was to get to the hospital to pick up his beloved Leona and bring her home. He had talked to a doctor—somebody—who had assured him he wasn't in any way hurt, only in shock, as was

to be expected. Much as he longed for it, there
was no way he could get to her until he had taken
care of everything that needed to be taken care of,
which was a great deal. He had heard the story, had
spoken to the police, had seen the television news.

Something was being hidden here. His instincts
over many long years had been honed razor sharp.
He turned the whole thing over and over in his
mind. He wouldn't believe a single thing until he
had Leona where she needed to be—safe in his
arms. From now on he wouldn't let her out of his
sight.

He parked outside the hospital in a doctor's
reserved spot, not caring. He didn't pause at reception. He swept on to the room where he knew
Leona had been taken. She wasn't on the bed. She
was sitting on a chair, fully dressed, her beautiful
hair cascading over her shoulders. It was the only
thing that looked vital about her. She was white as
milk, fragile as spun glass.

His heart melted with love. "Leo, sweetheart, I
came as quickly as I could." He went to her, raising
her with exquisite gentleness to her feet, keeping
his arms protectively around her.

She smiled at him. He had never seen a sweeter
more poignant smile in his life.

"Boyd," she said very quietly, reaching up to
stroke his cheek. "I'm *so* sorry."

"I know." He bent his head to kiss her. It was a

kiss that was more a solemn vow—an affirmation that she was his woman, the woman he was to marry. She was looking so traumatised it cut him to the heart. "Are you ready to go home?" he asked. "The car is just outside." He was desperate to hold her. Comfort her. Help her over her shocking experience. He knew he wouldn't be able to get over it.

"I go where you go," she said, raising her eyes to his. "I love you with all my heart. I'll love you until my last breath. What if I never had the chance to tell you properly?" She was suddenly frantic, feeling once more Rupert's strong ruthless hand at her back. "I can't possibly imagine life without you. You know that?"

"I do. I do. Hush now," he soothed. "You've had a terrible shock. I'm here. We're together. I'll never leave you. We're an invincible team, you and I. Now, let's get you out of here. We won't talk about anything until you feel you're ready."

The knowledge that he had guessed what might have happened flashed through her. How could she keep anything from Boyd? He always saw through to the truth. He saw behind the smoke-screen, even as part of him mourned the manner of his father's passing.

"He did save me in the end," she said sadly. "No secrets between us, Boyd?"

"No secrets," he confirmed, hugging her to him,

trying his hardest to crush the horror he felt a
what his father had seriously contemplated in
moment of madness, like some wicked god wh
demanded sacrifice. It didn't bear thinking about
Not now, though it would be with him all the day
of his life. His whole being was committed to com
forting his love, his only love—Leona.

"Only the two of us will ever know," she whis
pered.

He turned her to him. Kissed her. Their firs
public kiss. More loving kisses would be recorde
by the media over the many long years of thei
public life. Indeed it was to become near impos
sible for the public to imagine one without th
other. They were the Blanchards, not only
symbol of wealth and power, but wonderful hu
manitarianism and family love.

That early evening, with a momentous da
drawing to its close, Boyd and Leona walked arn
in arm down the long corridor, each gatherin
strength from the other. Those of the hospital sta1
who were about at the time smiled gently, compas
sionately at them. All were sensible to the fact tha
they were looking at two young people deeply i
love. The *real* thing was lovely, impossible to mis:

Rupert Blanchard's unhappy life was ove
Theirs had just begun.

EPILOGUE

TIDINGS OF JOY! RARE OLD TIMES!
Daisy Driver.
Aurora Magazine.
Place: Brooklands, the fab Blanchard estate
      in the beautiful Hunter Valley.
Occasion: The thrillingly spectacular Blanchard
         wedding.

EXCITEMENT REACHED FEVER pitch at the wedding
between the charismatic Boyd Blanchard and his
utterly enchanting bride, Leona, who won't have to
bother changing her surname. It was unques-
tionably the wedding—might I say celebration—of
the year. Take it from one who gets invited to these
things. The ceremony was held in the most romantic
of venues, Brooklands' famous rose gardens
brought to their peak for this wonderful occasion.

A dream temple was erected for the moving
ceremony—many a tear, me included, a virtual

torrent of sobs from someone behind me. For m
money, a union of *souls*—I've never been more sur
of anything in my life—the open air temple fille
with the bride's favourite flower, you guessed it, th
rose in all its beauty and bewitching scent.

The cream of society came from all over th
country. Dressed to kill. Lashings of bling.
whole contingent from overseas. The tab, I unde
stand, was picked up by the groom. Generous ma

The bride's dress made by our leading fashic
designer, Liz Campbell, also the bride's frien
was so ravishing I find it near impossible t
describe and I'm not one, as most of you wi
know, who is usually lost for words. But, for o
avid readers, I'll have a go. Take it for granted
was gorgeous as one would expect with such
gorgeous bride. Oh, that magnificent mane of re
gold hair and the luminous skin! Forgive me,
digress. The gown was strapless, moulded ski
tight to the body, dipping into the cleavage,
lustrous silk taffeta the colour of the eye-poppir
South Sea island pearls around the bride's throa
hand embroidered with ivory roses, as was a wic
band of the marvellously billowing skirt that shov
cased the bride's tiny waist. One had to see the e:
quisite fit, the detailing, that bell of a skirt th
became a short train to fully appreciate the effec
An elbow-length tulle veil was held in place by a
exquisite headpiece crafted with ivory ro:

ouquets, decorated with shimmering crystals and
ny pearls, the leaves quivering on tiny gold wires.
winging from the bride's ears—wait for it—were
ie fabulous Blanchard Diamond earrings, part of
suite I was told was acquired way back from a
outh African billionaire. What a family heirloom!
s the light hit them the female guests gave a col-
:ctive gasp. It took quite a while for me to lose the
etinal after-burn. Honestly, girls, there's *nothing*
ke an enormous diamond and when they weigh
1 at heaven knows how many carats it's a sight
our reporter will never forget.

Our beautiful bride had six bridesmaids in all,
ll stunning, all sliver-thin so they could get into
ie form-fitting long strapless gowns that echoed
ie lovely shades of the roses—porcelain pink,
lush pink, gold, soft yellow and an exceptionally
eautiful apricot. Such a colour palette perfectly
omplemented the bride's radiant colouring. Four
ttle flower girls from the Blanchard family, im-
ossibly pretty, in tulle and taffeta pale gold
resses with satin ribbons for headdresses with
ong flowing back bows attended the bride, along
vith two little pageboys, twins of the Blanchard
lan, who behaved remarkably well considering
vhat six-year-old tots can be like.

The groom looked absolutely splendid, girls. A
airy tale prince. Alas, now taken! Seriously, why
an't we all have a prince? His attendants had to

be a line-up of some of the handsomest and mos
eligible bachelors in the country. I don't like t
single one out—they all looked terrific—but th
bride's stepbrother, Roberto, who flew home espe
cially from his gap year stay with close relative
in Italy, is going to be a man to look out fo
Remember, I was the first to tell you!

The reception was held in Brooklands' magnif
cent ballroom. Out of this world! Some of you wi
recall the groom's beautiful mother Alexa, holdin
her famous charity functions there. Maybe we'
see the like again? Here's hoping! Anyway, th
food and drink—a bubbling fountain of Frenc
champagne—were sumptuous. I actually got t
dance with man about town, Peter Blanchard, wh
said nice things to me, and when prompted, abou
my column. I think he took a fancy to me becaus
I made him laugh.

Back in Sydney again and at my desk trying t
calm down after a magnificent over-abundance o
everything.

Of course one of these days I'm going to g
married too. No register office for me, girls, but
big, BIG, wedding, just like the Blanchards.

How rare and beautiful was that! I seriousl
doubt if I'll ever cover such a sublimely romanti
wedding again.

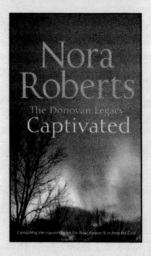

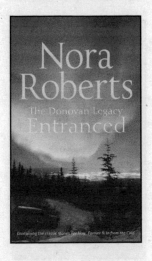

Passion. Power. Suspense.
It's time to fall under the spell
of Nora Roberts.

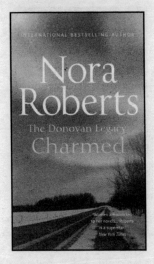

When Boone Sawyer came into her life,
Anastasia Donovan had to protect herself
and her magic at all costs.

Then she was confronted with a terrifying
threat. With a child's future at stake,
Anastasia could not deny her powers,
even if it meant risking her own life.

**This is the third volume in Nora Roberts'
spellbinding *The Donovan Legacy*.**

Available 6th March 2009

The Wedding Planners

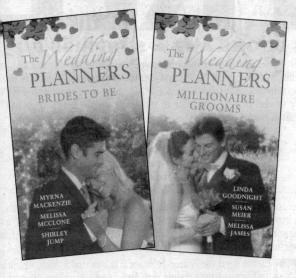

*Join these three
beautiful brides-to-be
as all their wedding
dreams come true!*

Available
16th January 2009

*These three lucky
ladies have a
millionaire's ring
on their finger!*

Available
20th February 2009

Planning perfect weddings…
finding happy endings!

www.millsandboon.co.uk

M&B